HIGH STAKES AT CASA GRANDE

A gambler down on his luck, Latigo arrives in town bent on vengeance. His aim is to ruin Major Lonroy Crogan, the owner of the town of Casa Grande, and then to kill him. With a loaned poker stake, he soon makes enough money to threaten Crogan's empire by buying up property. However, danger lurks on the horizon and Latigo's plans seem doomed to failure. Will he be forced to flee Casa Grande as an all round loser?

T. M. DOLAN

HIGH STAKES AT CASA GRANDE

Complete and Unabridged

LINFORD
Leicester

First published in Great Britain in 2007 by
Robert Hale Limited
London

First Linford Edition
published 2008
by arrangement with
Robert Hale Limited
London

British Library CIP Data

Dolan, T. M.
  High stakes at Casa Grande.—Large print ed.—
Linford western library
  1. Western stories
  2. Large type books
  I. Title
  823.9'14 [F]

  ISBN 978–1–84782–205–5

Published by
F. A. Thorpe (Publishing)
Anstey, Leicestershire

Set by Words & Graphics Ltd.
Anstey, Leicestershire
Printed and bound in Great Britain by
T. J. International Ltd., Padstow, Cornwall

This book is printed on acid-free paper

1

Jimpy Caan was a man who liked to study people. It exercized his mind while he earned a living tending horses. He regarded himself to be a shrewd judge of character. Maybe it was some kind of gift inherited from his Cherokee ancestors on his mother's side. But there was no skill in judging that the stranger riding in was a man down on his luck. Yet Jimpy was sorely puzzled as he watched the rider slow on reaching the first of the false-fronted buildings on the edge of town. There was a contradiction between the man and the horse. Though the rider wore store-bought clothes, they were frayed and threadbare and had long ago gone out of fashion. In contrast, the horse was a magnificent, gleaming black animal with a brilliant white star on its forehead. If Jimpy wasn't mistaken, which he never was when it came to horseflesh, the horse stood seventeen hands high. The saddle, hand-tooled and silver-studded, complemented the horse.

Spotting Jimpy standing outside of his livery stable, the stranger pulled the horse over to him and reined up. Dismounting with the stiff movements of a man who has ridden too far and too long without resting, he looked steadily at Jimpy through eyes that were startlingly blue. He took off his wide-brimmed Stetson that was caked with alkali dust, to reveal long fair hair that dropped to his shoulders.

Though solidly built, the stranger was of no more than average height. Around his middle he wore two gunbelts of dark leather with stout buckles. The butt-plates of the twin, holstered Colts were of beautifully polished walnut, another sharp contrast between the impoverished look of the man himself and his possessions. Apart from the Colts, only the newcomer's silver spurs were of any real value.

Moving to open the door of his livery, Jimpy said, 'Welcome to Casa Grande, stranger.'

Jimpy went inside, and the stranger followed him. Staying silent as he led his horse into the cool dimness of the stable, his eyes checked out every inch of his surroundings. Dropping the split reins, he did a slow quarter-turn to face Jimpy, studying him gravely.

When he spoke his voice was quiet and low. 'I'm looking to sell my horse, mister.'

'Wowee!' Jimpy exclaimed, shaking his head in wonderment. 'Any man has to have hit bad times before giving up his horse, but things sure must be real bad to part you from a magnificent mount like this here.'

Hard face registering no emotion, the stranger said, 'It ain't an easy choice. Thing is, if you don't buy him, I can't afford to pay you to water and feed him.'

'Well now!' Jimpy pursed his thin lips

3

to whistle his surprise. 'Like I said, things must be real bad, son.' He reached out to check the stallion's teeth. Bending to examine each hoof in turn, Jimpy then ran his hands slowly and appreciatively over the animal. 'Let me tell you how I'm fixed, stranger. I've been running this place for many a long year without becoming anything like rich. If I walked down to Barton Travers's bank right now and withdrew every cent I've got there, it wouldn't amount to a twentieth share in a horse like this, let alone that saddle and bridle.'

'I'm not asking for much. Make me an offer. I'll throw in the saddle and bridle.'

This had Jimpy scratch his chin thoughtfully and look shrewdly at the stranger. He took in the stranger's face. It had strength of character and good looks that caked dust and a few days' stubble of a beard couldn't conceal. After a brief scrutiny, he spoke. 'I ain't a man to pry into another man's private business, son, and it ain't a savvy thing to do in a frontier town like this. But I'm going to risk it with you. I'd say for certain sure that you is a gambler. And it's easy to see youse down on your luck, son.'

The rider nodded. 'It happens. I hit a bad streak in Wichita.'

'Then I hope that this town of ours changes your luck, son.'

'That can't happen if you don't buy my horse, mister.'

Rumpling his black hair as if the action helped him to think, Jimpy said impulsively, 'I have always been able to size up a man at once, stranger. I can't stretch to buying your mount, and I reckons as how I'm a fool with my money, but I'm sure enough ready to stake you twenty-five dollars.'

'I don't get it?' the stranger frowned, white dust cracking loose as his brow furrowed.

'Ain't every day you'll get an offer like it,' Jimpy chuckled, pleased with his idea. 'I'll take care of your horse and give him fresh water and oats for free, and stake you, twenty-five dollars to go in Lon Crogan's Lazy Horse Saloon and change your luck.'

'Looking at it from your side, it don't seem like much of a deal,' the stranger remarked.

After pondering on this for a moment, Jimpy explained. 'Even if they begged me sit at a card table, son, I wouldn't do it. I'm sure enough poor shakes as a gambler. That was something I learned years ago. I had myself this squaw once, see. Purty little thing she was, all set to be my bride. But there was this young buck by the name of Two Knives who wanted her, too. I wanted both her and money to set myself up in business when we married. So I bet her against a knee-high stack of fur pelts in a two-horse race. Two Knives won, and I got the pelts while Two Knives got the squaw. I set myself up with this livery stable, but never had no wife to share it. I ain't never placed a bet since. But I reckon as how I've always been some kinda gambler at heart. I'll be real happy if you double my twenty-five dollars for me.'

'If I don't, then my horse is yours.'

'No,' Jimpy declared emphatically. 'That ain't no part of the deal, son. If your bad streak goes on you'll keep your horse and ride out of here not owing me one cent.'

'You are a real gent, sir,' the stranger said.

'Real loco, most likely,' the ostler chuckled, holding out his right hand. 'Jimpy Caan.'

'Abel Latigo,' the stranger said, taking Jimpy's gnarled hand and shaking it.

An excited Jimpy hurried off into his private quarters. Still in a rush, he returned to hand twenty-five silver dollars to Latigo, who took it, saying, 'You've got yourself a deal, Jimpy. Tomorrow I should have this back to you plus interest.'

'There ain't no hurry, son,' the ostler assured him.

Running a hand over his stubble, Latigo remarked ruefully. 'I'd better go and get cleaned up and buy myself some clothes. A man has to look the part in my game.'

'Barber shop's just down aways, a block and a half on your right, Abel,' Jimpy advised. 'And you'll get yourself a good room and a tub to soak off that dust at the Cattlemen's Palace Hotel.'

'That will do me fine. What was the name of that saloon again, Jimpy?'

'You can take your pick of saloons in this town,' Jimpy chuckled. 'But I knows that most of the big games go on in the Lazy Horse.'

'And you say a man by the name of Lon Crogan owns it?'

The way in which Latigo checked the name of the saloon's owner sparked off Jimpy's overactive curiosity. A gambler new to a town would be interested in the saloon running the big money games, not the identity of the owner. Thinking it wouldn't be wise to question the stranger further, he said,

'Crogan owns the Lazy Horse and just about every gosh-darn thing around here.'

Accepting this with a nod, Abel Latigo put on his Stetson, touched the fingers of his right hand to the brim in a salute to Jimpy, and walked out of the stable without speaking another word.

★ ★ ★

A glowing cigar clamped between his teeth, Town Marshal Brett Steiner walked slowly and cautiously up to the batwing doors of the Lazy Horse Saloon. With a hand on each, he half opened them. Keeping back from the light from the lamps inside, he scanned the interior of the saloon, which was frantically alive. Games of faro, monte, roulette, blackjack, stud, chuck-a-luck, and fan-tan were in progress. A good-humoured crowd of miners, cowboys, and townsfolk with plenty of money that they were willing to spend were eager to try their luck. Saloon women wearing ruffled skirts and spangled bodices, were slowly circling, painted predators waiting to relieve the amateur gamblers of any money they might have left.

Close to fifty years of age, Steiner, like most big, powerfully built men, had reached his prime later in life than his peers. Though maybe slightly over the hill, he was still a force to be reckoned with. Casa Grande was wild, but he had tamed tougher towns in the past. Now, trading a lot on his reputation, he was paid good money for keeping law and order, while an income on the side came from turning a blind eye to the illegal practices of the man who owned the majority of the businesses and property, and who used intimidation to control the remainder.

Something of a dandy, Steiner was smartly dressed in a Californian-cut cord coat, a pale-blue shirt of fine broad-cloth, a silk waistcoat of brightly patterned colours, and tan-coloured riding pants.

He had survived a perilous lifestyle by spotting potential trouble before it became an actuality. This habit was made difficult by the sheer size of the Lazy Horse Saloon. There were three bars here on the ground floor. Straight ahead of him at the far end as he stood in the doorway, was a small stage with a piano standing on it. Flights of stairs ran up either side to a banistered landing from which doors led off to offices and private rooms. Making up the crowd were cowboys either from local ranches or straight in off the trail, some bearded and buckskin-clad scouts, hunters, miners, and a number of drummers who sat drinking and talking business.

Steiner was walking to the bar, his pace measured as he scanned the sea of faces. A sixth sense caused his body to tense as he spotted a stranger entering the saloon behind him. Well dressed and meticulously groomed, the man was a picture of elegance. As the doors swung back, the stranger unhurriedly crossed the floor. He wore a frock coat and a string tie. His wide-brimmed hat added an air of mystery by keeping the greater part of his face in shadow. The tinkling of the man's Mexican-made spurs of hand-forged silver was audible to Steiner's acute hearing.

Years of hard-earned experience warned Steiner that there would be a gunbelt with a holstered gun under the stylish frock coat. A gun that could quickly become a deadly weapon in the expert hand of the stranger. But the marshal had faced too many fast guns to be unduly worried. What concerned him most was the dominant presence of the man. His walk and manner exhibited what the marshal recognized as a carefully rehearsed air of humility and reserve. In spite of this, or, as Steiner suspected, because of it, the stranger stood out in the crowd. The marshal noticed that the people 'felt' the stranger's presence rather than saw him. Steiner had known very few men like that. All of them had been dangerous. Extremely dangerous.

The stranger headed for the poker table, and the town marshal decided against having a drink. The night was not going to run smoothly. Instinct told him to do his first patrol of the evening around the town, then return to the Lazy Horse to keep a watch on the stranger.

★ ★ ★

Used to the turning heads and speculative glances he attracted, Abel Latigo noticed the town marshal covertly studying him, and three men standing at the bar to the right of the card table. Constantly observant, they had the look of gunmen rather than wranglers.

Arriving at the table, Latigo stood watching the four players. The dealer was a thin man whose pale, hawkish face was given its only colour by the green eyeshade he wore. Beside him was an obese, elderly man whose clothing and manner oozed prosperity. The third player was a well-dressed young man, a business type; handsome and relaxed, seeming not to care whether he won or lost. Last of the four was a cowboy. His face, which was on the south side of ugliness, wore an intense expression that said he was desperate to increase his wages.

Watching the game with an expert eye, Latigo, his face impassive, felt the old, familiar excitement stirring in him. Gambling had been his calling ever since discovering that he was good at it while in the army. He checked for the signs of a dishonest game. There were none. Each time the dealer dealt it was a clean deal. The fact that the cowboy was winning didn't ease the fellow's stress. Latigo guessed that he was in urgent need of money. He could empathize with that, but deplored the cowboy's anxious state and jerky movements. A veteran player was careful to conceal any kind of feelings from his opponents.

14

Latigo pulled up a vacant chair, asking politely, 'Any objections to me buying in?'

The prosperous-looking man manipulated his fat, red face into a smile. 'I welcome you, sir. Even if you win, I won't lose, because your winnings will be mine come the morning.'

'Don't try to figure that one out, stranger,' the handsome man counselled Latigo in educated tones. 'This is Barton Travers, president of Casa Grande's bank.'

'Abel Latigo,' Latigo introduced himself, and Travers offered a podgy hand.

'Henry Whitsall,' the young man said as he, too, shook Latigo by the hand. 'If you're ever in need of anything from a pin to an elephant, or vice versa if you strike lucky tonight, you'll find my emporium on Main Street.' He indicated the cowboy with a sideways gesture of his head. 'I am unable to introduce you, as I don't know the name of our *compadre*.'

'Can we get on with the game?' the cowboy asked impatiently.

With a sad little shake of his head, Whitsall commented, 'That would seem to be the end of the introductions, Mr Latigo, as Connors, the dealer, tends not to socialize at the best of times.'

Taking his seat, Latigo waited. The final pot went to the cowboy, who was unappreciative enough to curse about the smallness of the amount.

Then the players settled back in their seats as the game began again. The cowboy's anxiety had him remain sitting stiffly upright. All five agreed table stakes and cards slithered across to them at speed. Eager hands reached out to pick up cards, give them a quick inspection then hold them, fanned out, close to the chest. A bottle of rye was on the table, and the banker pushed it and a clean shot glass towards Latigo. Pouring himself a drink, Latigo took time out from the game to enjoy the pleasant sensation given him by the full-bodied liquor.

He was surprised to discover that none of the other players had the coolness and concentration vital to a successful poker player. Their playing was erratic, disorganized. A period of more than two hours passed swiftly. Latigo's original ten-dollar stake had grown so that he was using the weight of several piles of dollar pieces to hold down a stack of paper money in front of him. In order to stay in the game, Henry Whitsall had given banker Travers an IOU for fifty dollars, and the scowling cowhand drank heavily as he watched his earlier winnings dwindling rapidly.

Alert as ever, Latigo had seen the town marshal leave the saloon earlier. Though there was no reason why they should be a threat to him, an intuitive unease had him keep a wary eye on the three gunslingers at the bar as he dealt the cards.

Unlike most of the frontier gambling fraternity, Latigo was a skilful player with no need to resort to dishonesty.

Holding the pack high, he sent cards expertly sliding to the other players. His style of dealing made it impossible to cold deck or bottom draw, so he was above suspicion.

He was placing the remains of the pack of cards in the centre of the table when the cowboy player, who was down to his last couple of dollars, nervously wet his lips and dropped his eyes. Glancing at Latigo, he turned nasty, saying angrily, 'I don't like this.'

His raised voice covered some distance and an expectant hush settled on the drinkers and gamblers close to the poker game. Those at the table looked at the cowboy aghast.

'What don't you like, *amigo*?' Latigo asked in his quiet, conversational way.

'That ... it's just that ... ' the cowhand blustered. 'It's just that ... it's just that before you sat in the game we were all winning some and losing some.' He stabbed a finger at Latigo's piled-up winnings. 'Since then you have been raking the *dinero* in.

How do you explain that, eh?'

'There's no call for this . . . ' Henry Whitsall began to complain to the cowboy.

Latigo interrupted him, asking in a cold tone, 'What do you mean by explain, mister? Are you suggesting that I've been cheating?'

'I think this has gone far enough,' Barton Travers told the cowhand. 'Now, you should apologize and leave us to continue the game.'

The cowboy, irate by then, suddenly exploded into action. His face a deathly white, he sprang up, kicking his chair back and going for his gun. He didn't clear leather. His body froze rigid as he found himself gazing into the dark muzzle of the Colt Latigo held in his right hand.

'Slow down, *amigo*,' Latigo drawled. He pointed to the two dollar pieces on the table where the cowboy had been sitting. 'Pick up what you've got left, then walk away.'

The cowboy was slowly reaching for

his money when one of the three men standing at the bar went for his gun, fast. But Latigo was quicker. Drawing his second gun with his left hand, he fired a shot that passed between an alarmed Travers and Whitsall. The bullet hit the gunslinger in the chest, throwing him backward across the bar before he'd even had chance to take aim.

As this happened the cowboy poker player took advantage of the distraction by pulling his gun. Re-holstering his left-hand gun, Latigo came up on to his feet in one speedy, fluid movement to crack the cowboy across the skull with the barrel of the gun held in his right hand.

As the poleaxed cowboy hit the floor hard, the injured gunslinger was being supported by his two companions. He was losing blood fast, and someone shouted, 'Get Doc Hendly.' But two companions picked him up and rushed towards the door. The crowd parted to leave a gangway.

'Oh, my Lord, Mr Latigo,' Whitsall gasped. 'You have just shot Rube Clements, one of Lon Crogan's top men.'

'Who had pulled a gun on me,' Latigo pointed out as he calmly stashed away his winnings. 'I guess our game has ended for this evening, gentlemen.'

A saloon girl was helping the cowboy to his feet, her painted face screwed up in horror as she saw the blood flowing redly from a gash in his scalp. He stood groggily, supported by a wall but liable to slide to the floor again if the girl stopped struggling to keep him upright.

'Perhaps you will give us the opportunity to get our revenge some other night, Mr Latigo,' Barton Travers suggested pleasantly, then observed, 'I think that you will shortly be otherwise engaged right now.'

Following the banker's gaze, Latigo saw that the crowd was now parting again. He caught a reflection of lamplight off a silver star a split second before he recognized the large figure of the town marshal heading his way. Stepping away from the table, Latigo stood waiting, ready to handle whatever was to come.

Stopping several feet away, Steiner stood with his feet placed slightly apart, body perfectly balanced and poised for action. The saloon had gone very quiet.

Henry Whitsall broke the silence by bravely speaking up. 'It was self-defence, Marshal.'

'I have already established that, Henry,' Steiner said. Then he addressed Latigo. 'Looks to me as if Clements is so bad hurt that Doc Hendly can't help him, stranger. We do things properly here in Casa Grande, so an inquiry into this shooting will take place. As a matter of form I ask to see the gun fired here this evening.'

'You agree it was self-defence, Marshal,' Latigo argued. 'That being so, I don't see it as right that you ask me to hand over my gun.'

'I'm not asking you to hand your gun

over, stranger . . . '

'The name's Latigo, Marshal, Abel Latigo.'

'I'm not asking for your gun to be handed over, Latigo, but I do want to examine the weapon for future reference at an inquiry,' Steiner explained in a reasonable tone. He pointed to the twin pistols on Latigo's hips. 'You have a second gun, so you will not be left defenceless.'

Nodding agreement, Latigo used a forefinger and thumb to grasp the butt of the Colt in the holster tied down to his left thigh. Extracting the weapon slowly, he made the town marshal visibly tense by slipping his fore-finger through the trigger guard. With his finger as a pivot he spun the gun clockwise, then reversed the spinning, keeping it going for a short while before sending the Colt twirling through the air at Steiner.

Steiner remained motionless as the gun hurtled towards him at great velocity. Just when it seemed that the speeding gun would strike Steiner hard, he took a short side-step to his left and effortlessly plucked the spinning gun out of the air with his right hand.

The perfection of the marshal's reflexes was not lost on Latigo as he watched him examine the Colt .45. It was a magnificently balanced weapon with delicately ornate chasing from the muzzle end of the barrel to the front and top of the loading gate. Raising the muzzle to his nose, Steiner sniffed it to make sure it was the weapon that Latigo had so recently fired. Having been told that Latigo had fired a gun held in his left hand, the marshal was aware that some men who wore two guns, and Wild Bill Hickok was one of them, usually drew diagonally across the body. Lowering it, he first hefted the Colt in his right hand before flipping the chamber out and trying it for twirl. Before clicking the chamber back, the marshal tested the amount of trigger-pull. Latigo's Colt was hair-trigger. This sensitivity, while highly dangerous for a novice, was vital for a man who lived by his gun.

Satisfied, Steiner spun the gun as Latigo had, sustaining the forward spinning for some time to keep Latigo guessing. The tension built among the spectators, and there was a concerted sigh as, at last, the Colt went rotating through the air at Latigo.

His natural reserve having him regret this show of gunplay, Latigo accepted that it was a necessary part of the marshal and himself sounding each other out. Unhurried and unflurried, leaning slightly to his right, he caught the gun with his left hand, re-energized the spinning, and then slid the weapon smoothly back into its holster. Taking a surreptitious glance at Steiner, he was rewarded by the sight of his pulse hammering hard in the lawman's throat. The marshal enquired, 'Let me buy you a drink, Latigo.'

As they walked to the bar together, Latigo was aware that Steiner had selected an unoccupied stretch of counter to avoid them being eaves-dropped. He ordered two whiskeys, and he and Latigo silently raised their glasses to each other.

'A wise man never objects to a friendly piece of advice, *amigo*,' Steiner remarked.

'Which I am about to receive,' Latigo guessed, smiling with the corners of his mouth.

'I hear tell that you struck lucky at poker here tonight.' Steiner's dark eyes looked over the rim of his glass at Latigo. 'Believe me when I tell you that you shouldn't ride your luck by staying around here. Ride out of town right now. Don't leave it until tomorrow.'

'I haven't broken the law, Marshal.'

'I'm not saying that you have.'

'All I did was shoot a man who drew on me.'

'Agreed,' Steiner nodded. 'But it wasn't just any man you shot, but one of Lon Crogan's top guns. The bad loser you pistol-whipped was a no-account cow-hand at the LC Ranch. Crogan doesn't

26

take kindly to such things. He's a big man in this neck of the woods; the biggest. Ranching, mining, saloons, freight business; you name it, Crogan's into it.'

'There's nothing you can tell me about Major Crogan, Marshal.'

Looking obliquely at Latigo, Steiner said, 'You must have the wrong man. I ain't never heard Crogan called Major.'

'I've got the right man,' Latigo insisted. 'I had the misfortune to serve under Major Crogan at Shiloh. Now, let me buy you a drink.'

Pushing his empty glass towards Latigo for it to be refilled, Steiner said, 'Then you'll be leaving town.'

'Reckon not.' Latigo shook his head. 'I'll be staying around here for a while.'

2

As Town Marshal Steiner rode in through the high-arched gateway of the LC Ranch, the cowpuncher, who appeared to be watering his horse at a nearby trough, watched him slyly. The innocuous look of the one-man-one-horse tableau didn't fool the marshal. The man was no cowboy. Lean and mean, he was one of Lon Crogan's hired guns. A business empire, comprised not only of most of Casa Grande but also the surrounding area, made a private army a necessity for Crogan, and no unknown or unauthorized person would be permitted to enter the ranch.

Ignoring him, Steiner rode on to approach the single-storey ranch house that took up a wide stretch of ground. He had no liking for what lay ahead. This visit to Crogan had been forced on the marshal by the death of Rube Clements, who had died during the night. Crogan, a cold and unfeeling man who cared little for his employees, would regard the killing as a personal affront. It would fuel his anger to learn that Steiner would not arrest the man responsible. Though he was on Crogan's unofficial payroll, the marshal scrupulously applied the law in serious matters. Latigo had shot Clements in self-defence, and Steiner wouldn't allow Crogan to push him into calling it murder.

Dismounting and hitching his horse to the rail, Steiner took a deep breath and stepped up on to the veranda. A gunslinger sitting there idly, a rifle lying across his knees, recognized him and allowed him to pass without a word. The door was open, and the marshal walked in to find Lon Crogan waiting for him. Sitting in an upholstered armchair that had projecting wings on either side of the headrest, Lon Crogan was a lightweight, a little man inflated by self-regard.

'Good morning, Marshal.'

Accepting Crogan's greeting with a curt nod, Steiner didn't speak. Though willing to accept a regular payoff from the businessman to further his own plans for retirement, he regarded the man with utter contempt. Crogan had an overweening belief in his own illustriousness. He was undoubtedly highly successful, but it was a success achieved through death and double-dealing. Ruling ruthlessly, he got what he wanted by means of a fast draw with a handgun or the crack of an assassin's rifle. It didn't shame Crogan that he was never the one to pull the handgun or squeeze the trigger of a rifle. He saw no wrong in paying others to do his killing for him.

'A drink?' he enquired of Steiner with a nod toward where a bottle stood on an ornately carved rosewood table.

Refusing the offer with a shake of his head, the marshal gave his bad news direct and without any preliminaries. 'Rube Clements was shot in the Lazy

Horse last night.'

'I know,' Crogan said. 'Luke Rodgers and Zeke Wiseman were with him, and they reported to me when they got back from town. How is Clements?'

'Doc Hendly did what he could, but Clements died in the early hours of this morning.'

'The boys told me it was some stranger gunned him down,' Crogan queried.

'That's right. He only hit town yesterday.'

'Well,' Crogan mused. 'Judge Hibbs isn't due for another five weeks, so keep the killer locked up. Maybe we'll wait for the judge, or maybe I'll get a mite impatient and arrange for my boys to deal with him one night.'

'He's not in jail. It was self-defence. Clements fired to protect one of your hands.'

Crogan made a short, lunging movement as if to get up out of his chair. Controlling himself with difficulty, he settled back down, his face made purple by rage. 'It's never self-defence when one of my men gets shot, Marshal.'

'There's a whole saloon full of witnesses to say different in this case,' Steiner said drily.

'Then just give me the name of this stranger.' Crogan's voice had a cutting edge to it.

Steiner hesitated. Abel Latigo may have been foolish in ignoring his advice to leave town, but he was the marshal's kind of man. That was something Lon Crogan would never be. Though he cherished the dream of having enough money to buy a small ranch and live quietly before his reflexes slowed and he fell victim to some young glory-seeking gunfighter, Steiner hated his liaison with Crogan a little more each day. The marshal considered that he had put his life on the line often enough to deserve an illicit pension, yet his nefarious activities always made him uneasy.

'He was a drifter who will probably be long gone by now,' the marshal said.

This vague statement didn't satisfy Crogan, but a door opening and Crogan's daughter Anna-Maria entering the room saved Steiner from further questioning.

There was absolutely no resemblance between father and daughter. Anna-Maria had a self-confident elegance that came from good breeding, whereas her father was simply arrogant. Crogan had been a widower when arriving in Casa Grande, and the marshal had always assumed that the girl took after her mother. There was something alive about everything that Anna-Maria did, all that she said. A lack of symmetry in her features defied a description of beautiful, but she was stunning. Dark-complexioned, her black hair, worn long, was pulled back and tied with a single ribbon.

'Good morning, Marshal Steiner,' she smiled. 'Don't let me interrupt anything.'

'Good morning, Miss Crogan,' Steiner responded, welcoming an opportunity to get away. 'I was just about to leave.'

'What was the name of the man you mentioned, Marshal?'

Steiner had reached the door when the innocent-sounding question from Crogan had him turn. Not wanting to give Latigo's name he realized he had no option other than to do so. Crogan would find out anyway.

'It's Abel Latigo,' Steiner said.

★   ★   ★

Latigo's first call that morning had been to the livery stable where he had passed Jimpy Caan seventy-five dollars. The ostler had protested vehemently. 'Lookee here, Abel. I'm more than happy to have doubled my money, not goshdarn treble it.'

'Take it. I had a good night,' Latigo had insisted. On his way out of the stable he had called back. 'Take care of my horse.'

'I sure will,' Jimpy had shouted a promise. 'He'll have ham and eggs for breakfast.'

Amused by this, Latigo strolled down the main street until he found the bank. A young teller behind the counter was eyeing him suspiciously when Barton Travers's plummy voice came from somewhere out of Latigo's vision.

'It's all right, Malcolm. I will attend to this gentleman.'

Travers's heavy figure came waddling into view. 'Mr Latigo. I was anticipating this visit with a considerable degree of pleasure, while at the same time dreading that it would not happen. I thought you might have ridden away from our fair town.'

'I'll be staying around for a while.'

'That is indeed good news,' Travers gushed. 'Now, please come into my office. I take it we have business to discuss.'

'We have,' Latigo confirmed as he followed the banker through a stained oak door.

Settling himself behind a massive desk after pulling up a chair for Latigo, Travers took a bottle and two glasses from a drawer. Placing them on the desktop, he poured a drink for Latigo and himself, while at the same time his piggy eyes didn't miss the stack of money that Latigo had placed on the desk.

'Here's to a relationship that is both prosperous and amicable,' Travers toasted, raising his glass.

'I'll drink to that,' Latigo responded. He nodded at his money. 'If my luck with the cards holds, this is the first of many visits I will be making to your bank.'

'Which is something I look forward to, sir,' the bank president enthused. Then he looked at Latigo thoughtfully. 'I do trust that you won't consider this to be a transgression, Mr Latigo. Obviously you are a gambler, but I get the impression that you might have a hankering to set yourself up in business here in Casa Grande. Am I right?'

'Possibly,' Latigo shrugged. 'But the way I hear it, one man has the whole business shebang just about hog-tied.'

Raising one bushy eyebrow, Travers said, 'Mr Crogan.'

'How do you see Crogan, Mr Travers?' Latigo enquired.

'As a highly valued customer, highly valued. Mr Crogan puts a tremendous amount of business through the bank.'

Fixing Travers with a steady stare, Latigo drawled. 'That's your opinion as a banker. How do you see him as a man?'

'My dear fellow,' Travers stammered, his small eyes oscillating violently for a second or two. 'That direct question puts me in something of a quandary. If I give an equally as direct answer, do I have your word that it will go no further than these four walls.'

'I've always accepted that a conversation between a bank and a customer is strictly confidential, Mr Travers.'

'Of course. Of course.' Travers nodded and could not stop his head nodding for a short while. 'I can say without fear or favour that Mr Crogan has a fine reputation here-abouts as both a gentleman and a businessman.'

'But?' Latigo prompted.

Travers had to summon up a reserve of courage before replying. 'The fact is, Mr Latigo, that Mr Crogan encroaches on the business of my bank.'

'In what way, Mr Travers?'

'To gain his own ends. It is all but impossible to purchase any property in these parts other than through Ringstead's Real Estate. Ben Ringstead, ostensibly the owner of the business, is nought but a front man for Crogan.'

'And Crogan provides loans for the buyers?' Latigo guessed.

'Exactly, through Ringstead and at very high interest rates,' Travers confirmed, setting off another spell of uncontrollable nodding. 'Crogan's way is not my way, Mr Latigo. In addition to the Ringstead activities, he has gained many businesses here by lending the original owners money at extortionate rates, then foreclosing when the borrower is unable to repay the loan. Under a cloak of respectability Crogan conducts his business in a deplorable manner. I dread the day when Casa Grande is completely in his grasp. Might I enquire as to your interest in this man?'

'Let's just say that I have a score to settle with Crogan.'

'And?'

'I could really use your help.'

'You will have it, providing it in no way prejudices the bank, nor in any way becomes a threat to my staff.'

'You have my promise on both counts,' Latigo affirmed. 'But I would like to establish myself here in Casa Grande before we discuss it further, Mr Travers.'

'That is your prerogative,' Travers concurred.

'But we must not let business interfere with pleasure,' Latigo said with a hint of a smile. 'I will be running a card game in the Lazy Horse tonight. Can I expect you to be there?'

'As I spend my days dealing with wholly predictable facts and figures, Mr

Latigo,' Travers replied, 'to have some-thing of value rest on nothing more than the turn of a card provides me with immeasurable pleasure.'

'That's something I can understand.'

'There are others like me in town, of course. I will put the word around, and look forward to seeing you this evening, Mr Latigo.'

★ ★ ★

The sky was a low ceiling of dark clouds that morning, darkening the world to a depressing grey for Henry Whitsall. With the day's business just beginning, he was rolling the last barrel of grain into place outside of his store when he heard the uneven sound of his sister's foot-steps on the board sidewalk.

'Exactly how much did you lose, Henry?' asked Verity Whitsall, her tone sharp.

Using both hands pressed into his back to ease the strain, Henry straight-ened up from his task. He nervously faced a normally placid Verity. Lame from birth, she stood favouring her defective right leg while she awaited his answer. With the complexion of a redhead, skin as white and smooth as alabaster, she had a unique loveliness that attracted the men of Casa Grande. But Verity wasn't interested. Her whole life was devoted to her brother and the general store they ran together. That was her vocation. Verity's avocation was helping Pastor Morrish at his church.

'Not much,' he replied ashamedly.

Had it not been for the killing of Rube Clements, she wouldn't have known he had been in the Lazy Horse last night. He hated deceiving his sister, but it was impossible to live up to the standards that she set. Whether or not she found it easy to live like a saint, Verity clearly believed everyone else could do the same.

Waiting to join him in saying 'Good morning' to a small group of passing townsfolk, she returned doggedly to her question. 'Exactly how much?'

41

'About seventy dollars,' he answered, not mentioning that amount had included a fifty-dollar IOU to Travers the banker.

'Henry, how could you!' Verity exclaimed in horror. 'You know that we need every cent we make in the store.'

What she said was true, but was also absolutely pointless in Henry's opinion. They had borrowed money to buy the store three years ago. Despite it being a thriving business, they still struggled to pay the interest without even having started to pay off the loan.

'Whatever we make in the store it will never be enough, Verity,' he said in an attempt at reasoning with her. He went on to give a simple analogy that increased his guilt because he knew it was an insult to her high intelligence. 'It's as hopeless as trying to fill a pail that's got a hole in the bottom. My reckoning is that if I play the occasional hand of poker I'm sure to get lucky some time soon. Then we'll have enough money to take care of every-thing.'

She shook her head, making the mass of red hair swing. 'People like us can't depend on luck, Henry.'

Verity was right. He had to admit that, first to himself and then, when he could find the courage, to his sister. Even when he did win at poker, he was so mediocre a player that the pot didn't come anywhere near making up for his previous losses. Because he enjoyed the game he had been foolishly chasing a dream while lying to his sister. He would never win enough at cards to cure their financial problems. But he had to get her to face facts, too. Though they both worked hard each day, they would never break free from debt.

Henry was reluctantly about to acquaint her with this unpalatable truth, when he noticed that two cowpunchers riding slowly by had turned their heads to look at something or somebody across the street. As they rode on by he saw the object of their attention. News about the shooting of Rube Clements had travelled fast, even to the outlying ranches. Walking along the sidewalk across the street with the relaxed but ready-to-spring movement of a mountain lion, was Abel Latigo. As he passed people on the street it was obvious that he was the main topic of conversation that morning.

Catching sight of Henry, the elegantly dressed Latigo came across the street. 'Good morning, Henry.'

'Good morning,' Henry responded, made to feel boyishly awkward by his sister's presence. He turned to Verity. 'This is Mr Latigo. We met last night. Abel, my sister, Verity.'

'Pleased to meet you, Miss Verity,' Latigo greeted her, taking off his wide-brimmed hat and giving a little bow.

Henry could see that Verity was impressed by Latigo's gentlemanly behaviour, but knew that this was outweighed for her by the knowledge that he had killed a man last evening.

Though his sister had forced herself to endure the violence and sudden death of a frontier town, she had never been able to tolerate it, let alone accept it. Many of Pastor Morrish's fire and brimstone sermons on the subject had been penned by Verity's fair hand.

'Maybe it's early in the day to speak of such things, but I've set up a game for tonight at the Lazy Horse, Henry,' Latigo said. 'Barton Travers will be sitting in. I guess that I'll see you there.'

Pausing, Henry waited in anticipation of Verity stating emphatically that he would not be there. That would be a terrible humiliation for him to suffer in front of a man such as Abel Latigo. But a few seconds later he was scolding himself for believing that his sister could do something like that. She would never shame him in public, but he was keenly aware that she was now expecting him to reject Latigo's invitation firmly.

'We're mighty busy here at the store

right now, Abel, what with the book-keeping and all,' he began, wordily leading up to an insipid refusal. 'I don't allow that I'll be able to spare the time.'

'I'd like you to make it if you can, Henry,' Latigo said amiably. He gave Verity another little bow, said, 'Nice to have met you, Miss Verity,' replaced his Stetson on his head, and walked off in his lithe way.

'I'd prefer it if you would keep away from that man, Henry,' she said, softly but earnestly, as she walked with Henry back into the store.

'I was there, Verity. Latigo had no choice other than to draw on Clements,' Henry protested in defence of the man he admired.

'Perhaps not,' she assented. 'But there is something about him that frightens me. Tell me you won't be playing poker with him tonight, Henry?'

Not appearing to have heard her question as he lugged a heavy sack of potatoes across the floor of the shop, Henry made no reply.

★ ★ ★

It was still early evening, but the Lazy Horse bars were all doing good trade when Abel Latigo made his casual entrance. A pianist up on the small stage was pounding out a night-herder's song for a group of appreciative cowpunchers. Business was booming and the saloon girls were smiling happily when he passed through the crowd to order a drink at the bar. Picking up a news-sheet he was idly leafing through it but, never off guard for one moment, saw Barton Travers come in through the batwing doors. Though to any observer Latigo would appear to be totally immersed in the news-sheet, he watched Travers look around, seeing him standing by the bar, and head his way.

The big-bodied banker bellied up to the bar, his florid face shining from his recent ablutions. Scanning the crowd, he gave a two-word response when Latigo bought him a drink. 'Most gracious.'

'Could be a good night,' Latigo remarked as the two of them raised their glasses.

'Indeed, indeed,' Travers agreed. 'Do you see that gentleman standing watching the roulette with a somewhat hungry eye?'

Taking in a tall, thin man with a carefully shaped moustache and dark, pomaded hair, Latigo nodded.

'That, my dear Mr Latigo, is Benjamin Ringstead,' Travers said. 'Let him stew among the money-changers for half an hour, and he'll be chomping at the bit, so to speak, for a game.'

Glancing at the barkeeps who were under pressure and sweating, Latigo asked 'I'm told Lon Crogan owns this place.'

'That is indeed correct, Mr Latigo,' Travers confirmed. 'The Lazy Horse was the first property acquired by Crogan when he arrived in the district. Jess Wheeler, who owned the place then, ran into trouble in a card game with Crogan. The game had gone on between Jess and Crogan for about an hour, with Jess hardly getting a look in. With nothing left but the saloon, Jess was desperate enough to bet it on what was to be the last game. They were sitting at that corner table over there by the stairs. It sure seemed that the cards had begun to fall Jess's way at last in the opening hand of the new stanza. It looked like all he had to do was reach for that pile of money in the centre, and Crogan would be riding out of Casa Grande for good, a broken man.'

'I guess that wasn't the way it happened,' Latigo remarked.

Shaking a sad head in remembrance, Travers enlightened him. 'Jess laid down two cold pairs and was reaching for the pot. I'll swear that a large part of Jess Wheeler died right there and then when Crogan laid down a full hand on the table.' Travis looked wistfully around him before continuing. 'This place is the centre of Crogan's domain; the rock upon which he built his empire. Strange thing is, he walked out of here that night as the new owner, and has never set foot in the place again.'

'I never had Lonroy Crogan figured as a gambler,' Latigo mused aloud.

The sharp-minded banker picked up on this at once. 'So you know Crogan?'

'Met him a long ways back,' Latigo admitted. 'Like I said earlier today, I aim to get established here in Casa Grande. Maybe I'll tell you then.'

★   ★   ★

Back upright in the saddle, Anna-Maria Crogan handled her horse with the nonchalant style of an expert rider. She passed into the shadows of some pines from where she saw the last ray of sunlight snatched over the horizon. The sun had gone and long shafts of sullen light poured through rolling country-side and the jumbled silhouettes of the distant town of Casa Grande. There was a sultry feel to the air, a breathless heat that she hoped the approaching night would cool. Otherwise the atmosphere inside the town's small concert hall would be unbearable.

As she reached the long, level and straight trail leading into Casa Grande, Anna-Maria didn't turn in the saddle to look back. There was no need to. Somewhere back there, most probably just out of sight, would be the two gunslingers sent by her father to avenge the death of Rube Clements. She had never liked the uncouth Rube Clements, and she loathed Rodgers and Wiseman, the two hard men her father was sending into Casa Grande, even more. She guessed that a part of their duty would be to watch over her that night.

Though accepting that her father's obsessive concern for her safety was little more than a rich man's concern for his daughter, Anna-Maria's innate strength of character had gained her at least some freedom from her father's domination in every other respect. He didn't approve of her meeting Barry

Cleat that evening, but knew better than to try to stop her. Barry was more cultured than all but a few of the men in and around Casa Grande. Tonight he was taking her to see a group of itinerant players' version of John Howard Payne's play *The Fall of Tarquin*.

As she entered the south end of the town's main street and saw Barry Cleat's large premises up ahead, Anna-Maria was reminded of the main cause of her father's dislike for the man. Barry was in the freight business in opposition to one of her father's enterprises. With a sharp eye for business, Barry Cleat was something that Lon Crogan couldn't tolerate: a serious rival.

He was waiting for her. Wearing a dark grey suit and a brilliant white Stetson, he looked and behaved as a perfect gentleman, helping her dismount and providing an arm in support as she stepped up on to the sidewalk. One of the boys employed by him came out to take care of her horse.

'Seems like it could be a full house, Anna-Maria,' Cleat remarked, as couples and small groups passed them on the way to the concert hall.

'The play had an unusually long run in New York,' Anna-Maria said, 'so it must be really good.'

Pastor Morrish and his wife, accompanied by Verity Whitsall, went by, exchanging civil 'Good evenings,' as they did so. The elderly Dr and Mrs Hendly each waved a hand to her and Barry from the other side of the street. The two Williams sisters, who owned the haberdashery store, smiled shy greetings as they passed by arm-in-arm.

This was a community at leisure, completely in harmony with itself. It made Anna-Maria feel good to be involved in it. She had already begun to enjoy the evening immensely.

Barry Cleat, his face made even more handsome by the subtle shades of twilight, asked gallantly, 'Will the most beautiful woman in Arizona do the luckiest man in Casa Grande the honour of taking his arm?'

'With pleasure, kind sir,' she responded with a smile.

Life couldn't have been more perfect for Anna-Maria as they strolled towards the concert hall. With the shadows deepening and the street illuminated only by the flickering lights of the saloons and hotels, there was something very special in the air. As they went in through the doorway she turned her head to take one last look at the magical scene.

A sudden chill ran in a wave through Anna-Maria's body, and the spell of that night shattered as she saw her father's two hired guns dismounting further down the street. Being the daughter of Lonroy Crogan meant that, no matter how much she tried, she could never become a part of the community.

3

Henry Whitsall paused and took a deep breath to strengthen his resolve before using both hands to push open the batwing doors of the Lazy Horse. He eased a feeling of guilt by reminding himself that he had promised his sister only that he would not play poker. Verity would never deny him the pleasure of a quiet drink. But his gambler's instinct picked up the tension of a card game that had Abel Latigo, Barton Travers, Ben Ringstead and a rancher named Deacon as players. The fifth player came as a surprise to Whitsall. Holding a hand of cards close to his chest was Town Marshal Steiner, who was almost as renowned for his miserly attitude towards money as he was for his formidable skills as a fighting man.

Slowly crossing the floor, Whitsall

was conscious of the pulses in his throat and temple throbbing wildly as the old excitement surged up in him. Fighting the urge to sit in on the game was difficult, but he managed to secure a truce with himself if not a victory.

Determined to remain a spectator, Whitsall wandered closer to the table, offering up a silent prayer that Ringstead, who regularly took just about every hardearned cent from Verity and him, was losing heavily.

But with none of the players able to make anything out of the cards that turned up, the play was lamentably weak. Whitsall neared the table without any of the gamblers affording him a glance, but he was certain that the watchful Latigo was aware of his arrival. Things began to change gradually as Whitsall continued his observation. The cards began to fall better, and the bets were rising accordingly. To Whitsall's chagrin, the luck was favouring Ringstead, an impassive-faced, cool and skilful player.

During the second part of the game, Latigo started an apparently reckless method of over-betting. Having sat at the table with Latigo the previous night, Whitsall accepted that there was nothing careless about his seemingly clumsy play. It was a strategy that had him quickly recoup his losses. What must have been close to an hour passed by, with Latigo's run of luck holding. The marshal and the rancher dropped out and became interested spectators. Travers was showing signs of nervousness, but Ringstead calmly lit a cigar and resumed play once he had a comfortable halo of smoke around his pomaded head.

Henry Whitsall was very conscious of the fact that he was watching a serious, perhaps momentous event slowly unfolding.

★ ★ ★

The drama taking place on stage was brilliantly acted and enthralling, but

Barry Cleat's inability to concentrate ruined his enjoyment. A different, real-life drama was running disturbingly through his mind. Anna-Maria had been unusually withdrawn since they had entered the theatre, and he had questioned her on this during the interval between scenes. Though always loath to discuss, or even admit to, her father's ruthless business methods, she had reluctantly revealed what was worrying her. Anna-Maria was convinced that her father had sent Rodgers and Wiseman into town that evening to avenge the death of Rube Clements. Like Cleat, Anna-Maria knew Latigo only by name, and Cleat had solicitously pointed this out to her.

'As it is Spanish for a strap used to fasten a saddle, I would say Latigo is not his real name. He is probably just a drifter, Anna-Maria,' he had advised. 'There is no way in which you can be held responsible for him.'

Thoughtful for a moment, she had replied, 'If I do nothing to prevent him from being killed, then I am every bit as responsible for his death as my father will be.'

'No one who knows you associates you with any of your father's actions,' Cleat had protested.

'Maybe not, but I am his daughter,' had been her flat and inarguable answer to that.

Now, as the play moved towards its climax, Anna-Maria leaned close to Cleat to whisper a request. 'When the show ends, Barry, will you find this Latigo person and warn him?'

'Is it worrying you that much, Anna-Maria?'

'I just can't let it happen,' she said unhappily.

This put Cleat in a quandary. As a rival of her father, he had no wish to hasten the inevitable day when the immensely rich and powerful Lonroy Crogan forced him out of the freight business. Even so, he was desperate to help Anna-Maria. Though she would appear to be as composed and confident as ever to anyone else, Cleat could tell that she was seriously troubled. So he suggested a compromise. 'Perhaps the wisest thing for me to do is tell Marshal Brett Steiner about this.'

'There is no point in that,' Anna-Maria responded scathingly before voicing her opinion of Steiner. 'It was the marshal who came out to the ranch this morning to tell Dad who had shot Clements.'

The rumour that Steiner was Crogan's man had grown stronger of late, although no one was foolish enough to whisper a word of it within earshot of the much-feared marshal. Aware of this, Cleat accepted Anne-Maria's contention that it would be pointless to involve the town marshal. He was left with no option but to do as she requested.

'If Latigo's in town I'll find him,' Cleat promised her. 'But only on one condition.'

'What's that?'

Nodding to where Verity Whitsall sat

beside Pastor Morrish and his wife, Cleat said, 'I want you to go home with the Whitsall girl and stay there until I come for you. That way I'll know that you will be safe.'

'If that's what you want, I will stay with Verity.'

'Is that a promise?' Cleat asked earnestly.

'That's a promise, Barry.'

★   ★   ★

Ringstead had made up his earlier losses in the game, and was again getting ahead. Unperturbed, the deceptively watchful Latigo was putting together in his mind the pattern of the system that Ringstead was using. A super-confident bluffer, the real-estate man consistently opened up the pot with a wager large enough to suggest that he was holding a good hand, even though he wasn't. Latigo lost money in support of his studied pretended ignorance of the method of play

Ringstead was using.

Without in any way revealing that he was wise to Ringstead's system, Latigo scooped a sizeable pool with a flush of spades. He followed this up with another win so large that it had put Travers out of the game. Ringstead beckoned to a bargirl to order more whiskey for those around the table and some Havana cigars for himself. Before the girl returned, Latigo had drawn a reasonable pot on three of a kind.

Whitsall watched Latigo's steady hands roll a cigarette, while Ringstead poured himself a large drink and downed it in one. This was a sign that suggested to Whitsall that the real-estate man was losing his nerve, but he was as cool as ever when play resumed. But that was soon to change.

With Latigo studying him with half-closed eyes through the smoke of his cigarette, Ringstead's play became gradually more wild, more erratic. It was plain to Whitsall that Ringstead, despite his Casa Grande reputation as a skilled poker player, had never sat across a table from anyone of Latigo's class. As time passed he bet heavily and unwisely on bluffs, and let excellent chances pass him by. When something over one and a half tension-filled hours had gone by, he was in deep trouble.

At the next start of play, Ringstead began cautiously. He had some small successes but was by now edgy. He had lost a lot more than any man in his position could afford to lose. Whitsall guessed delightedly that the real-estate man was now betting with Crogan's money. The consequences of that were guaranteed to be disastrous. Ringstead's undoing came from being unable to adjust to losing. Desperate to get back into the game on a sure footing, he overreached himself and Latigo had him cold. Staring hard into Ringstead's eyes, Latigo caught him with an acehigh full house.

Looking unbelievingly at the huge pot Latigo was raking in, Ringstead, his voice a little shaky muttered, 'That's me.' He poured himself a long drink, and spoke in flat, measured tones after drinking it. 'This is a first for me, Latigo. But there will be other nights.'

'There will be,' Latigo promised softly. 'I aim to be around here for quite a while.'

Standing up from the table, Ringstead forced himself to make a dignified exit from the saloon, holding his head high. Henry Whitsall left shortly after him, eager to find Verity and tell her that the hated Ben Ringstead had lost heavily. Deacon, the rancher who had been in on the game, had gone earlier. Barton Travers had been his heavily pleasant self when he went. Latigo was left alone with Marshal Steiner, for the first time that evening he became aware of the marshal as a person and not just a player in the game.

Reaching for the whiskey bottle, the marshal refilled Latigo's and his own glass, then spoke conversationally. 'Ben Ringstead lost a whole heap of money tonight, Latigo, and he's a Lon Crogan man.'

'Meaning?'

'Meaning that you have made yourself a right powerful enemy,' Steiner said. 'The way I see it you're doing that deliberately. You're intent on waging some kind of war against Crogan. Isn't that so?'

'Maybe Crogan started it in another war a long time ago,' Latigo replied enigmatically.

'That don't make no sense to me, Latigo.'

'I didn't intend it to, Marshal.'

Emptying his glass and refilling it, Steiner looked at Latigo speculatively. 'You once mentioned that you knew Crogan. At Shiloh, wasn't it?'

'That's right.' Head down, Latigo stayed quiet for a while as he deliberated. He liked Brett Steiner, and decided that he owed it to the marshal to talk straight. 'I was a sergeant at Shiloh, and Crogan was my commanding officer. He proved that he had a yellow streak a mile wide, Steiner, and I lost ten good men due to it.'

Letting his breath out in a low whistle of surprise, Steiner said, 'I never had Crogan figured as a coward. I sure guess that's enough to have you hate him.'

'Not only for Shiloh, but Chicamauga, too.'

'What happened there?' The marshal cocked a quizzical brow.

'Same sort of thing. The major pulled foot and I lost another six men, including my young brother.'

Whistling softly again, Steiner's tone was both sympathetic and concerned. 'That's an almighty burden to carry through the years, Latigo. I can appreciate any man's need for revenge, but I ask that you understand my position. I can't stand aside and let you fight Shiloh and Chicamauga over again here in Casa Grande.'

'I'm not here to cause trouble, only to play cards, Marshal,' Latigo assured Steiner.

'Playing cards had you kill one man your first night in town, Latigo.'

'The other *hombre* drew first.'

'Even so,' the marshal said with a slow shake of his head, 'I have you down as a gunfighter first and a gambler second.'

'Maybe, maybe not,' Latigo responded with a casual shrug. 'Are you trying to tell me something, Marshal?'

Steiner nodded. 'Could be that I am. I like your style, Latigo. Probably if we'd met a few years back we would have become *amigos*. But if you start any gunplay here in town, against Crogan or anyone else, then you'll have to face me.'

Latigo spoke easily. 'That's not how I reckon on playing it, Marshal. It will be a real slow, long game during which I intend to relieve Crogan of everything he holds dear.'

'Money,' Steiner said.

'That, and power.'

'But not his life?'

'Oh yeah. That will be the last thing

that I take. But it will be done all lawful-like.'

Steiner pushed his glass away and stood up from the table abruptly.

'Time to do your rounds of the town, Steiner?' Latigo enquired conversationally.

'No, Latigo. It's just that I don't never think it right to drink with a man I may have to kill,' the marshal replied tersely before turning his back on him.

Latigo watched the marshal make his way to the door. Steiner's walk was as graceful as that of a cougar, and there was a natural self-assuredness in every move that he made. If the marshal's prediction of a showdown between them came true, Latigo was aware he would be facing his equal. Possibly even his better.

★   ★   ★

Stepping back from where he had been looking into the smoke-swirling interior of the Lazy Horse Saloon, as the doors were pushed open and Henry Whitsall came out, Barry Cleat asked, 'Do you know what this drifter named Latigo looks like, Henry?'

'Sure do,' Whitsall affirmed, squinting curiously at Cleat in the half-light. He turned to look in over the half doors. 'That's Latigo sitting at that table with Marshal Steiner, Barry.'

'Thanks,' Cleat said, as Whitsall paused, continuing to show his curiosity before turning to stride off down the street.

Moving closer to the doors, Cleat watched the marshal stand up, exchange a few words with Latigo then move off towards the door. Stepping into the shadowy area at the side of the door, Cleat waited for the marshal to come out and pass by.

But Steiner took one step out on to the boardwalk and stopped. Looking straight ahead, his arms relaxed at his side, his hands still, he spoke. 'Whoever you are, hear this. Show yourself or I'll gun you down.'

Astonished by Steiner's perception, Cleat found that an ominous dimension had been added to the dark night. Made nervous by what he accepted as a very real threat, Cleat stepped out into the yellow glow of the lights from the saloon.

'Barry Cleat.' Steiner identified him in a surprised tone. 'Now why would you be skulking around in the shadows trying to get yourself killed?'

'I was looking to have a word with the man called Latigo,' Cleat stammered.

'That's another way of getting yourself killed, Cleat.'

'I don't get your meaning, Marshal Steiner.'

Sighing, the marshal turned to face him. 'I'm saying that Latigo killed one of Lonroy Crogan's top hands. You are walking out with Crogan's pretty daughter, so you wanna impress her daddy by evening up the score.'

'You got it wrong, Steiner,' Cleat retorted angrily. 'I wouldn't give Crogan the time of day, and Anna-Maria wants me to warn Latigo that her father's sent a couple of guns into town to bushwack him.'

'I know you well enough, Barry Cleat, to believe what you say,' Steiner said. 'But you are a businessman not a gunslinger, so you shouldn't get yourself mixed in with this sort of thing. Latigo can take care of himself, and don't need a warning of any kind.' The marshal paused to look over the top of the batwing doors into the saloon. 'Here comes Latigo now, so you do as you think fit, Cleat.'

Moving off down the sidewalk, the marshal was swallowed up by the darkness as the saloon doors pushed open and Latigo came cautiously out into the night. Cleat immediately recognized that Latigo was no aimless drifter. There was something special about Latigo, a personal magnetism that reached out through the darkness and held Cleat. His body tensed a little as Latigo looked suspiciously at him.

'You got some kind of problem, mister?' Latigo asked in a low but challenging tone.

Determined to keep his promise to Anna-Maria, Cleat said, 'My name's Barry Cleat, and I'm here with a friendly warning. There's a couple of Crogan guns in town looking for you.'

'Who are you, and why are you telling me this?' Latigo enquired.

His eyes scanned the dark street as if it was daylight. Before Cleat could reply, Latigo took a step back into the shadows that Cleat had recently vacated. He spoke in an urgent whisper. 'Get out of the light, pronto.'

Ready to obey, Cleat couldn't be sure whether the report of a six-gun, incredibly loud in the night, happened first, or he was struck a terrific blow in the back before hearing the sound of the shot. Knees giving out, he pitched forward and would have hit the sidewalk if Latigo hadn't grabbed him under the arms to keep him upright. Pain seared through his back and his chest then. Aware of something warm and sticky on his back, he realized that he was bleeding badly.

Involuntarily drawing in huge breaths, he found that he was unable to breathe them out again. His lungs, filled to bursting, seemed about to explode. A blackness was creeping through his head as he felt Latigo lowering him into a sitting position on the boardwalk, with his damaged, bleeding back propped against the front wall of the Lazy Horse saloon.

Latigo's silhouette was bending over him, and Cleat tried to say something to him, even though he knew not what. Instead of words leaving his mouth there was a sudden gushing of blood as his tortured lungs erupted.

His pain increasing, Cleat was aware that Latigo was saying something to him, but the words were indecipherable blurred echoes inside his head. Knowing that he was badly injured he longed for a loss of consciousness to blot out the agony of his wound, while at the same fearing losing control of his senses.

Lowering himself on to one knee beside the injured Cleat, Latigo took off his spurs and left them on the board-walk against the wall of the saloon. Then he moved soundlessly away. A childish panic at being left alone gripped Cleat as he saw Latigo move away to disappear into the darkness.

Latigo's hope was that the man who had shot Cleat didn't know that he had got the wrong man. Should that be the case, he would be careless now. If not, Latigo was at a disadvantage. Cleat had warned that there were two of them, and everything was in their favour. They would be approximately aware of where he was, but he had no knowledge of their location.

The sound of footfalls on the boardwalk had Latigo pull into a narrow passageway between two buildings. Drawing a gun with his right hand, he waited. His tension eased as he recognized the unmistakable outline of Jimpy Caan slowly passing within a few feet of him.

Taking a chance, he whispered, 'Jimpy.'

'Gosh darn it, Abel,' Jimpy whispered back, surprising Latigo by identifying his voice. 'Ain't you got no regard for a fella's nerves?'

'I need your help, Jimpy.'

As an excuse for having stopped, the astute Jimpy pretended to be scraping something off his boot on the edge of the boardwalk. His whisper was just audible. 'Is this to do with two of Crogan's guns, Abel?'

'Yes.'

'Do I have a choice in this?' Jimpy asked with a little chuckle. 'If so, you can have your money back.'

'This is no time for fooling, Jimpy.'

'I allow that you're right, Abel,' Jimpy whispered in reply as he scraped imaginary mud off his other boot. 'Luke Rodgers and Zeke Wiseman sure ain't the kind of *hombres* I'd fool with.'

That had to be the names of the men Crogan had sent into town to get him. Latigo asked tersely, 'Have you seen them, Jimpy?'

'I have, Abel,' Jimpy confirmed. 'Theys holed up down the street aways. Them two work a high and low routine, Abel. One of them stays at ground level while the other sets himself up high in a building.'

'Do you know where they're at right now, Jimpy?' a grateful Latigo asked.

'They ain't going to let you get back to the hotel, Abel. There's a freight wagon left outside of Fin Svengliss's place. Luke Rodgers is holed up behind that, but darned if I can tell where Zeke Wiseman is, but sure as shootin he'll be up on a roof or suchlike.'

Preparing to move off, Latigo said, 'Thanks, Jimpy. Do me another favour, *mi amigo*. You'll find an injured man called Cleat outside the Lazy Horse. Check on him, and if he's alive fetch a doctor to him.'

'I'll do that, Abel,' Caan promised.

'Barry Cleat's a good man.'

When Latigo started to make his cautious way down the street, a mist had settled to put his surroundings slightly out of focus and make things normal appear to be unpleasantly eerie. After covering some twenty yards, he saw the foggy bulk of a freight wagon across the street. By narrowing his eyes he could just make out the sign on the building behind the wagon: *F. Svengliss Barber Shop*. That was where Luke Rodgers would be waiting. The location of Zeke Wiseman, the second Crogan gunslinger, was the problem.

Pausing in an area of deep shadow, Latigo picked up one single and insignificant sound. At first it meant nothing to him. Then he found himself trying to place it without knowing why. Intuition had always played an important role in his life, and now it was urging him to concentrate. It had been a dull, metallic sound. He waited for it to occur again, but it didn't. In a split-second everything came together in his head. The sound had definitely come from the low, timber-built church just ahead of him. It had a bell-tower that was not high, but it was tall enough to permit a direct bead on anyone in the street. The man up there must have inadvertently collided lightly with the bell.

Running the few yards towards the church, Latigo was proven right when a bullet chipped wood splinters from the wall beside his head, lacerating his right cheek. Crashing in through the church door, blinking away a half-blindness brought on by the weak interior lighting, Latigo saw a figure at the altar turning to him in shock. It was a man who, though darkly clothed, was of gentle appearance. In the deep and practised voice of a preacher he called censoriously to Latigo.

'Bring not the weapons of death into the house of the Lord, sinner. I am Pastor Morrish. Leave, young sir! Go now before you incur the wrath of the Lord.'

Moving past him, Latigo headed for the small but sturdy door into the tower. There was a twisted wrought-iron loop for lifting the latch, but he had no time. Raising his right leg, he kicked the door open. It thudded against the inner wall as a cry of outrage came from the direction of the altar.

Standing at the foot of a rickety spiral staircase, holding a Colt in his right hand, Latigo discovered that the tower was much less lofty than he had pictured in his mind. Able to clearly see the single bell, he could just make out the shadowy figure of a man. With a rifle to his shoulder, Zeke Wiseman was peering down into the dark stairwell trying to see something to aim at. Latigo wasted no time in squeezing the trigger.

There was a deafening boom from the bell as the Crogan man's rifle flew out of his hands and hit it. The rifle was falling fast and Latigo had to take a sideways step to avoid it. Then the gunman was half-slithering, half-tumbling down the twisting staircase. Rolling the last few steps, he landed on his back at Latigo's feet. From the blood darkly staining Wiseman's homespun shirt, Latigo knew that his bullet had caught him in the left side a little below the heart.

Lifting his eyelids the wounded man looked at Latigo through eyes that were startlingly blue. Dropping to one knee beside the man, Latigo heard a rattling in Wiseman's throat and saw his head fall to one side.

Latigo was about to stand up when he became aware of a pair of gaitered legs beside him. Looking up he saw the grey figure of Pastor Morrish standing there, looking down forlornly at the dead man.

'Is the man dead?' he enquired in a hoarse whisper.

'Yes,' Latigo confirmed.

'Oh, Lord! The church has been defiled.' The dour clergyman's eyes flamed. 'Stay where you are, young man. I must seek and find Marshal Steiner.'

Taking Latigo by surprise, Pastor Morrish dashed for the street door of the church. Realizing what was happening, Latigo leapt after him. Morrish was going out of the door by the time Latigo was able to grab the shoulder of his jacket. He was about to pull the clergyman back inside when the harsh sound of a rifle being fired came from across the street.

A bullet chipped the door jamb just inches above Pastor Morrish's head before Latigo could pull him inside and kick the door closed.

4

Hearing the sound of a single gunshot behind him after leaving the saloon, Henry Whitsall cautiously retraced his steps up the street. A few yards from the Lazy Horse, he was standing trying to identify a figure that was stooping over something slumped against the saloon wall, when the loud ring of the church bell farther down the street startled him. It also caused the stooping figure to come upright. Henry saw that it was Jimpy Caan.

'It's all right, Jimpy, it's me,' Whitsall called.

'You skeered me, Henry,' the hostler complained. 'Why in tarnation is that bell ringing at this time of night?'

Discovering that the sound had reached the place partway down his spine that fear made act up, Henry was ashamed. 'I don't know.'

'Could be the death knell,' Caan contemplated.

'What d'you mean, Jimpy?' Never having had much to do with Caan, Henry always regarded him as a strange, eerie person.

'Take no notice of me, boy. It's just me Cherokee blood talking. But I'm glad that you're here. I need a hand with this fella. He's been hurt real bad.'

Walking over to see a man slumped on the boardwalk, Whitsall was about to ask who it was when he recognized Barry Cleat. The freighter was unconscious and losing blood fast. Whitsall shakily enquired. 'What happened to him, Jimpy?'

'He got shot,' Caan answered cryptically. 'Come on, give me a hand lifting him up.'

'Where we going to take him?'

'Some place. Any place as long as it's away from here. We gotta get Doc Hendly to take a look at him.'

Whitsall made a quick decision. 'Let's take him to my place.'

'That's fine. Like as not he'll be dead afore us gets there,' Caan gloomily predicted. 'You take his shoulders and I'll take his legs. It'll be best if we can get to your store by keeping off the street as much as possible.'

* * *

A frown of puzzlement on her pretty face, Verity Whitsall exchanged glances with Anna-Maria Crogan. Both women were disturbed by the single clang of the church bell that boomed through the night to reverberate inside the walls of the cramped living quarters at the back of the Whitsall store. During the time they had been together the atmosphere had become increasingly difficult, the conversation more and more stilted. Anna-Maria accepted that the fact that they belonged to different sections of society placed an invisible barrier between the lame girl and herself. Verity had struggled all of her life, working hard and battling against all the misfortunes that beset the poor. In contrast, and Anna-Maria was prepared to admit it to herself, as the daughter of a wealthy man she had never known hardship. The only thing that she and Verity had in common was a liking and respect for each other. That wasn't enough to produce subjects for small talk to pass away anxious waiting hours.

Nerves on edge, she had sipped coffee and nibbled biscuits automatically, even managing an occasional smile despite the desperation of her situation. She had made a terrible mistake when asking Barry Cleat to intervene. He was a businessman and not a fighting man, and would be no match for her father's hired guns. Also, the stranger named Latigo was an unknown quantity, and could well be as much a threat to Barry as Rodgers and Wiseman.

'What is happening, Verity?' Anna-Maria asked as the hollow booming of the bell faded.

'I don't know,' Verity replied. 'Pastor Morrish was going to the church when we left the theatre, but that doesn't explain why the bell rang.'

'I'm really worried about Barry,' Anna-Maria confided. 'He should have been here long ago.'

Verity stood and walked towards the kitchen, saying as she went, 'I'm sure that he'll be here soon. I'll make us some more coffee while we are — '

She broke off at the sound of the urgent hammering of a fist on the rear door of the premises. The faces of both the women were strained as they looked fearfully at each other.

★   ★   ★

There was only one way in and out of the church, and Rodgers had the door covered from across the street. Latigo realized that his situation was desperate. Having considered taking up the dead Wiseman's former position in the bell tower, he had cancelled it out as pointless. From that angle he could not draw a bead on Rodgers, who would be crouching behind the wagon. Standing at his side, Pastor Morrish had been shocked into silence by his close encounter with a rifle's bullet. In the knowledge that to escape from the church would require assistance from the clergyman, Latigo made a careful approach.

'I need your help, Pastor.'

Body still trembling from his frightening experience, Morrish took a long time to answer. 'I realize that, my son. You have killed a man, and I will give you all the help I can to have you come to terms with that.'

'First I need your help to get us out of here.' Latigo ignored the offer of spiritual help and stressed the priority. Slipping his left-hand gun from its holster, he held it out to Morrish. 'Take this, Pastor.'

Shrinking back from the weapon, Morrish regained some of his composure and courage. 'I have never touched a firearm in my life, and you will not force me to do so now. I have to leave now. Mrs Morrish will be waiting for me.'

'She'll have a long wait, Pastor,' Latigo remarked. 'We have no chance of leaving here unless you help me.' Holding the gun close to the clergyman so that he could see it in the poor light, Latigo demonstrated how to fire it. 'I'm not asking you to kill anyone, Pastor. All I want is for you to go up in the bell-tower, point the gun across the street, high up, and shoot holes in the air when I call up to you.'

Bewilderment rather than agreement had Morrish fumblingly take the gun. But he remained stubbornly immobile. Left with no alternative, Latigo reached with one hand for the door latch, and caught hold of the shoulder of the clergyman's coat with the other. Opening the door slightly, he dragged Pastor Morrish towards the gap.

'I'm going to push you out, then make a break for it while he's shooting at you, Pastor,' Latigo said tersely. 'Unless you do as I say?'

Eyes bulging with fear, the clergyman was in such a state that he ripped his coat as he struggled to get away from Latigo. Not liking what he was doing, but having no choice, Latigo forced the clergyman back to the door. He knew that he had to press home the advantage that terrorizing Morrish had given him. Though he could never bring himself to carry out his threat, he couldn't let Morrish suspect that he was bluffing.

Opening the church door wider, he made as if to push the clergyman out. Then he pulled him back swiftly and kicked the door closed as the rifle across the street was fired and a bullet buried itself into the thick wood of the door. It was too much for Morrish.

'I'll do as you say,' he gasped.

Latigo steered Morrish round the body of Zeke Wiseman and took him to the bottom of the spiral staircase. Pressure from one hand on his back had the clergyman start reluctantly up the stairs.

'Remember, start firing as soon as I call to you,' Latigo instructed as he picked up the rifle dropped by Wiseman. 'Don't let me down, Pastor.'

Going to the church door, he carefully lifted the latch. One hand still on the door ready to open it, he called up to Morrish. 'Start shooting.'

Minutes that seemed like hours went by without anything happening. Resigned to his plan having failed. Latigo guessed that Morrish had either decided not to obey now that he was no longer being menaced, or he had not got the hang of using a six-shooter. Wracking his brains for another idea to flush Rodgers out from behind the wagon, Latigo came up with nothing other than to leave himself open to the Crogan gunslinger by stepping boldly out into the street.

About to do this, he halted as Morrish fired a single shot up in the tower. This wasn't enough, but then there came the crack of another shot, and then another. Anticipating that Morrish would now continue until the gun's chamber was empty, Latigo went out of the door in a crouching run.

Under cover of the firing up in the bell-tower, he went halfway across the street and then dropped flat to the ground. In the faint light from a starlit sky he saw an unaware Rodgers moving to the end of the wagon nearest to him. The Crogan man was getting himself into a position to fire up at the tower. His back was to Latigo, who, breathing a little sigh of thanks, held Wiseman's rifle up to his shoulder and took aim. Ready to blast Rodgers, he found that he was unable to backshoot a man.

He called, 'Turn around, Rodgers.'

Swinging round to face Latigo and bring a handgun to bear on him, Rodgers stood no chance. Latigo squeezed the trigger and the rifle exploded, discharging its shot noisily. The heavy slug slammed into the Crogan gunslinger's chest, lifting him off his feet and sending him flying backwards, arms and legs akimbo. The unmistakable sound of breaking, splintering glass filled the street as Rodgers collided with the barbershop window.

Standing, holding the rifle so that it pointed at the sky, Latigo walked to shattered window. Having died instantly, Luke Rodgers lay on the floor of the shop, his clothing and body slashed in a score of places by shards of glass.

Aware of soft footfalls approaching, Latigo swiftly brought his rifle down at the ready. But it was Marshal Steiner who appeared out of the night to stand beside Latigo and look into the barbershop.

'You sure attract trouble, Latigo,' Steiner commented mournfully. 'I heard the shooting. Who was backing you up in the church tower?'

'You sure you want to know, Marshal?'

'Probably not, but I have to ask.'

'Pastor Morrish.'

A dismayed Steiner groaned. 'I wish that I hadn't asked.'

★ ★ ★

With Anna-Maria close behind her in support, Verity had nervously opened the door in response to the frenzied knocking. Both women had jumped back in alarm as Henry Whitsall and Jimpy Caan had come stumbling and staggering in, both exhausted by carrying the injured Barry Cleat. Doc Hendly, a small, elderly man with quick movements and intelligent eyes, had come in behind them.

'What has happened?' a distressed Anna-Maria asked demandingly, but got no answer.

Now, with Barry Cleat lying on Henry Whitsall's bed, blood leaking from him fast to soak the bedclothes on which he lay face down, the two distressed women were still no wiser as to how Cleat had been hurt. Doc Hendly, though disadvantaged by his advanced age, was working fast on the gaping gunshot wound in Cleat's back. Stemming the flow of blood by pressing a pad hard against the injury, the doctor instructed Caan and Whitsall to turn Cleat on to his side. Verity and Anna-Maria gasped on seeing the exit wound of the bullet. On the right side of his chest, it was not so large or gory as the hole in Cleat's back, but the horror of it lay in its proof that a rifle bullet had passed right through the body.

While the doctor had deftly bandaged the still unconscious Cleat, Anna-Maria repeated her question. 'What has happened to Barry?'

Jimpy Caan answered. 'Seems as how he got shot in mistake for Abel Latigo, Miss Crogan.'

'Do you know who shot him, Mr Caan?' Anna-Maria questioned.

'Couldn't tell yuh, miss,' Jimpy mumbled uncomfortably.

'He can tell you but he doesn't like to, Anna-Maria,' Henry said firmly. 'We met Marshal Steiner on the way here, and Jimpy told him that it was either Zeke Wiseman or Luke Rodgers.'

Taking an involuntary backward step, eyes widened in shock, Anna-Maria was grateful for the comforting arm that Verity put around her. Aware that she was directly responsible for what had happened to Barry Cleat, she was distraught.

'Where are Wiseman and Rodgers now?' Verity asked.

'Most likely getting ready for a long stay on Boot Hill,' Jimpy told her with a grim little chuckle. 'Last I saw of Latigo he was going after that pair, and I sure as shootin' wouldn't want Abel Latigo to come after me.'

'That man,' Verity exclaimed bitterly. 'He's been nothing but trouble since he arrived in Casa Grande.'

'Tis t'other way around, Miss Whitsall,' Jimpy objected. 'Casa Grande has given Latigo nothing but trouble since he got here.'

Stepping back from the bed to look

down at his patient, Doc Hendly shook his head despairingly and his eyes misted over as he visited that far place of reminiscence that is only accessible to the aged. 'When I settled here this was a great town to live in. That varmint Lon Crogan has spoiled everything.'

'Will Mr Cleat be all right, Doctor?' Verity asked so quickly that Anna-Maria was grateful to her for trying to minimize the effect of the old doctor's mistake in criticizing her father within the hearing of his daughter.

Deliberating silently for a few moments, the doctor then replied 'I've stopped the bleeding, but he's lost a lot of blood, Verity, too much for me to be confident that he will recover. I will be back in the morning when, hopefully, after he's had a night's rest his condition will allow me to be more positive.'

'I'll sit beside him all night, if you will permit me, Verity,' Anna-Maria said. 'After this, I cannot go back to my father tonight or at any other time.'

'You are welcome to stay here as long as you like, Anna-Maria,' Henry Whitsall said gallantly.

Peering at him speculatively over the top of his spectacles, Doc Hendly cautioned, 'You may soon regret making that offer, young Henry. Crogan is not the kind of man to take desertion by his daughter lightly.'

'Then I'll stay tonight but leave in the morning,' Anna-Maria decided. 'I don't want to put Verity or you in danger, Henry. Don't worry about me. I'll find somewhere to stay.'

'You won't be safe either in Casa Grande or beyond,' the doctor warned.

'I won't defend my father. I can't defend my father,' Anna-Maria declared. 'But I am confident that he would do me no harm.'

'I'm not suggesting that you are in any physical danger,' the doctor explained. 'But he will make life hard for you. Be wise, Anna-Maria. Go home in the morning and make as if what happened to Cleat tonight has made no difference

97

between you and your father.'

'That will be difficult, if not absolutely impossible, Dr Hendly.'

'Nevertheless, it is something you must do,' the doctor told her gravely.

* * *

'What sort of a man would take a life inside of a church?' Pastor Morrish asked the question hollowly as he walked up to Latigo and Steiner.

Pointing to the body of Rodgers lying among the ruins of the barbershop window, the marshal replied laconically, 'The same sort of man who did this to a barber's shop, Pastor.'

Seeing the body lying there for the first time, the clergyman recoiled, praying fervently in a whisper until Steiner interrupted him. 'Don't waste your prayers on this *hombre*, Pastor. Barry Cleat sure could do with your help in that direction. Either this hired gun or his *compadre*, who Latigo gunned down in your church, shot

Cleat in the back tonight. I'm sorry that your church was used, but put the blame for that on Lon Crogan, not Latigo.'

Studying Latigo in the poor illumination of starlight for a few moments, Pastor Morrish said, 'So you are this Latigo there's been so much talk about. Marshal Steiner has persuaded me that you are not to blame for the ghastly occurrence in my church. You had no choice, I understand that now.' He turned to Steiner. 'You say Barry Cleat has been hurt, Marshal. Is he at Dr Hendly's house?'

'No. I met Henry Whitsall and Jimpy Caan carrying him to the Whitsall place. The doc was following close behind.'

'Cleat will have need of me,' Morrish murmured sadly. 'I pray that I shall be in time.'

'I'll come with you if I may, Pastor,' Latigo said. 'Cleat was shot in mistake for me.'

'Your company is welcome, my son,' Pastor Morrish responded.

★ ★ ★

Billy Kline, foreman of the LC Ranch, spun round as the door of his room at the end of the bunkhouse opened. It was past midnight and Kline, who had been preparing for bed, knew that a visitor at that time wasn't likely to be on a friendly mission. He reached to the end of the cot where his gunbelt hung. Pointing the gun at the doorway, he lowered the weapon swiftly on recognizing the caller.

It was his employer, Lon Crogan, who spoke in his usual abrupt manner. 'Have you been in town tonight, Kline?'

This question immediately put Kline on guard. Though he hadn't been in Casa Grande, several of the hands had. They had returned with news that Wiseman and Rodgers, Crogan's two top guns, were dead. Though Crogan had to know, Kline didn't want to be the one to tell the formidable ranch owner. Having long ago earned a reputation as a hard man, Kline wasn't afraid of Crogan in any sense other than fearing for his job.

'No, Mr Crogan,' he replied respectfully.

'Some of the boys must have been in Casa Grande,' Crogan reasoned. 'Do you know who they were, Billy?'

The use of his first name didn't fool Kline, it alerted him. When appearing to be friendly, Crogan was either at his most devious or most dangerous. Even so, Kline accepted that he now had to come clean. If Crogan questioned his cowboys, there would be dire consequences should one of them let slip that they had told Kline that Wiseman and Rodgers had been killed.

'I heard some of the hands talking earlier, Mr Crogan, and it's bad news,' Kline said nervously.

'How bad?'

'Zeke and Luke have been shot.'

'Hurt bad?'

Rapping out like pistol shots, Crogan's two-word questions unsettled Kline. He was aware that to continue delaying the news that Wiseman and

Rodgers were dead would backfire. Knowing how disastrous that would be, he answered. 'Both Wiseman and Rodgers are dead, Mr Crogan.'

Kline watched Crogan's tanned face whiten quickly and dramatically. The ruthless Crogan had made many enemies, a fact that had had him rely on Wiseman and Rodgers for security. Though there were other gunslingers in Crogan's employment, none was anything like as efficient or as fast on the draw as the two men who had just been killed.

'How did it happen?' Crogan tersely enquired. His eyes were horrible little black beads.

'The way Bud Honeygan, he was one of the hands in town, was talking, the same man who shot Rube Clements gunned down Zeke and Luke, Mr Crogan. Some stranger who goes by the name of Latigo.'

'Who is this Latigo?'

'I don't know, Mr Crogan.'

Turning to leave, Crogan paused, as

if from an after-thought, to ask casually, 'Did any of the boys mention seeing Miss Anna-Maria in Casa Grande tonight, Billy?'

This was a strange question for Crogan to ask about his daughter, and Kline was unsure how to answer. When managing to reply he stammered a little. 'No, Mr Crogan. I can go in the bunkhouse and enquire if you like.'

'No,' Crogan replied, then spent a few moments in thought. 'No. There's no problem. I'll see you in the morning.'

'Yes. Goodnight, Mr Crogan.'

Not responding, Lonroy Crogan went out of the room, closing the door behind him.

★　★　★

Verity Whitsall accepted that her mind was playing some trick on her. But that realization didn't help her. Doc Hendly had left, to be replaced by Pastor Morrish, Marshal Steiner, and Abel

Latigo. Though this crowded the small room it normally wouldn't have worried her. She identified Latigo as her problem. By no means a big man, he nevertheless seemed somehow to fill the room, leaving her no space in which to move, to think, to breathe.

Both Latigo and the marshal had enquired after Barry Cleat's condition, the former remorsefully admitting that Cleat had been shot in mistake for him while delivering a warning that Wiseman and Rodgers intended to kill him.

Anna-Maria asked, 'Have you see anything of Wiseman and Rodgers tonight, Marshal?'

'Sure thing. Miss Crogan,' Steiner replied gravely, then introduced Latigo. 'This is Abel Latigo, a newcomer to Casa Grande. Latigo, meet Anna-Maria, the daughter of Lonroy Crogan.'

The glance the marshal exchanged with Latigo was not lost on Verity, but she was mystified by it. Anna-Maria had noticed, and appeared to be as puzzled as Verity was.

'Both of those men are dead, Anna-Maria,' Pastor Morrish announced. 'They were attempting to kill Mr Latigo.'

'Did you shoot them, Marshal Steiner?'

Anna-Maria had asked the question, but Verity anxiously and impatiently waited for the marshal to reply. She found herself offering up a silent prayer that it had been Steiner who had done the killing. Since Latigo had arrived in the room her brother had been regarding the man with adulation or, more accurately, hero worship. Maybe she was being ridiculous, she thought, but she would feel safer for Henry and herself if Latigo hadn't killed someone yet again. The man was bad for the town, and a bad influence on her brother.

'No, Miss Crogan, I didn't. The two men had laid a trap for Abel Latigo, and it was he who shot them.'

'With my assistance, I very much regret to say,' Pastor Morrish made a shockingly unexpected confession.

Stunned into incredulity, Verity Whitsall gasped. 'No, Pastor Morrish, that cannot be so.'

'I'm afraid that it is, Verity. I now fully accept that Mr Latigo had no choice other than to take the action that he did, and the circumstances were such that I had no option but to assist him. I came within a hair's breadth of being killed myself.'

'Oh dear, Pastor Morrish,' a dismayed Verity said breathlessly.

Anna-Maria spread her arms out in a gesture of helplessness. 'All this is really terrible, and I will understand if none of you wants me here.'

'Don't be silly, Anna-Maria,' Verity chided her.

'Don't get me wrong when I say this, Miss Crogan,' Marshal Steiner began, then continued hesitantly. 'You are highly regarded around here, and no one in this room feels any animosity towards you. Having said that, considering the hour, I think that to avoid bringing trouble upon yourself you should head back to the LC Ranch at once.'

'But,' Verity strongly protested. 'Anna-Maria can't be permitted to ride all that way alone at this time of night.'

Henry Whitsall immediately volunteered. 'Don't worry, Verity, I will be happy to escort Anna-Maria to her home.'

'Indeed you won't,' his sister said adamantly.

'Verity is right, Henry,' Steiner agreed with the worried girl. 'Things could turn real nasty if Crogan's got men out searching for his daughter.'

'Never a truer word spoken,' Jimpy Caan piped up.

Overruled and outnumbered and humiliated, a blushing Henry Whitsall accepted the verdict of those around him. He joined most of the others in the room to turn and gaze expectantly on Marshal Steiner. But it was Anna-Maria who made her thoughts on the matter clear.

Having at least partly recovered from learning that Barry Cleat had been shot, she was now very much her old, somewhat haughty self. 'Your concern for me is very much appreciated. However, I assure you that I will be quite safe riding alone.'

As Verity was seeing her to the door, Latigo moved closer to Steiner to ask softly, 'In what direction does the LC Ranch lie, Marshal?'

'You did well getting Wiseman and Rodgers tonight, but don't ride your luck, Latigo,' the marshal advised.

'Not telling me won't stop me, Marshal. Telling me will just make things easier.'

5

The mist had cleared and a cloudless, starry sky showed Latigo a well-worn track uncoiling ahead of him, winding its way like a drab-coloured ribbon through the rolling, treeless terrain. Coming upon a stream bubbling crystal clear from between rocks, he knelt beside it to splash the cool, invigorating water over his face. Refreshed, he drank deeply before moving on.

The night offered a solitude that he was keen to embrace. It eased away the remaining tension in him caused by the earlier gunplay in Casa Grande. Marshal Steiner had verbally and reluctantly directed him to the trail leading to the LC Ranch. The marshal had deliberately refrained from asking Latigo why he was taking the trail. If he had enquired, then Latigo would not have had an answer. Meeting

Crogan's daughter had presented him with a challenge that was as yet unformed in his mind. Did he see her solely as a means of connecting with Lonroy Crogan? He doubted that. Stunningly attractive, she had inherited none of her father's obvious character faults, except that she had a superior attitude that Latigo had found off-putting while at the Whitsall home.

Rounding a spur of volcanic rock he became instantly alert. Something had moved in the shadows up ahead, too close for anything to be gained by dismounting and making a cautious approach. Reining in close to the rock, Latigo squinted his eyes and was able to distinguish a horse standing listlessly up ahead, its head drooping. A woman stood beside the animal. It had to be Anna-Maria Crogan.

Moving his horse forward at a walk, Latigo's guess was proven right. Her head high, Anna-Maria was looking steadily at him without any trace of fear at being alone with a stranger in what was virtually a wilderness. Coolly surveying him, she leaned one shoulder against her magnificent stallion. All that betrayed what was perhaps an underlying uncertainty in her was the way she tossed a whip from one hand to the other as he approached.

'He went lame,' she said cryptically as an explanation of how she came to be standing there.

Nodding, Latigo dismounted. Sitting on his heels beside the stallion, he grasped a fetlock and lifted each of the animal's hoofs in turn. Still holding a back leg, which had a loose shoe, he was about to look up to tell her so when he felt something cool against his chin.

It was the tip of her whip, and she applied pressure to bring his face up so that she was looking down into it. Her white teeth sparkled in the starlight as she smiled and said, with the inflection of someone who was perplexed. 'We meet again. You are Latigo, the stranger who has caused so much trouble in town.'

Her interest in him was clear to read in her eyes. Latigo would have readily responded to it, no man alive could fail to be affected by such a woman. But his reason for coming to Casa Grande took precedence over all else, and he averted his gaze.

'I'd heard of you, of course, before you came to Verity's home,' she was saying, still keeping the whip firmly against his chin. 'But I didn't expect to meet you.'

'No doubt we move in different circles,' he remarked, raising a hand to move the whip away from his face so that he could straighten up.

'We can't be sure,' she said. Then sarcastically added, 'I saw John Howard Payne's *The Fall of Tarquin* at the theatre tonight. Perhaps you were in the audience.'

She was looking at him as if he was some kind of animal she was considering purchasing at a livestock market. Latigo took exception to her manner. He didn't intend to permit her to talk down to him. Keeping his irritation in check, he said coolly, 'Had it been *The Merry Monarch* I would have been there. That is a much better play, but, of course, Payne had the help of Washington Irving when writing it.'

Taken aback by his knowledge of the arts, she was speechless for a few minutes. There was a touch of temper in her made evident by the way she rhythmically beat the whip against her thigh. Then she quickly recovered her poise. 'You are a rarity out West, Latigo. You are possibly able to read and write to some extent, when most around here can do no more than make their mark.'

'I can make my mark, Miss Crogan,' he boldly assured her.

Looking away from him she murmured something in such a low voice that Latigo had to strain his ears, and even then he couldn't be sure. It seemed to him she had complimented him by saying to herself in a whisper, 'You have already made your mark.' Then she raised her voice to ask, 'Can you help with my horse?'

'No, miss,' Latigo slapped the stallion lightly on its flank. 'He will need walking home.'

'Damn,' she cursed, unladylike, her heavy lips thinning a little.

Putting a foot in the stirrup, Latigo mounted up. 'You can ride up behind me, Miss Crogan, if your dignity will permit.'

'Come now, Latigo, there is no call for a display of cynicism,' she mildly rebuked him. 'You have gone out of your way to impress upon me that you are intellectually superior to the dullards I have to tolerate daily. If the circumstances were different, I would ask my father to employ you.'

She raised her right arm and he leaned over in the saddle to grasp her wrist. Pulling her up on to his horse, he commented bitterly to himself, 'Circumstances would need to be very different.'

'Did you say something?' she asked.

'No,' he lied, moving his horse off

with her horse pacing along with them, its partially detached shoe making a regular clinking sound.

'We have less than two miles to go,' she told him.

'Do you feel safe out here in the night with a stranger, Miss Crogan?' Latigo enquired conversationally.

Before she could reply, a night bird disturbed by their approach came up out of some brush to their right. Climbing almost vertically, its song had the sound of angels in it. They both watched it until the bird was no more than a speck, and its delightful song had to be imagined more than listened to. Neither of them said a word, but it was a shared moment so profound that it would live on in each of them.

Then she answered his question over his shoulder, her face close to his. 'No one remains a stranger to me for long.'

They stayed quiet until they rounded a low hill to enter a miniature valley. A few hundred yards ahead was the arched gateway of a ranch. Anna-Maria whispered the word 'Stop' in his ear, and pointed.

Pulling his horse to a halt, Latigo followed her pointing finger. Sitting on a rock in front the gateway was a man, obviously one of Crogan's hired hands waiting for Anna-Maria to come along the trail.

'Let me down from the horse, Latigo,' she said quietly. 'Then you must go, as quietly as you can. I can walk my horse from here. Thank you for helping me, and God speed.'

Noticing the change that had come over her since seeing the man lurking up ahead, Latigo accepted that knowing he would be less than welcome on her father's property, she was protecting him. Lowering her gently to the ground, he paused for a moment. Though physically free of the woman he remained tethered by an invisible cord to her compelling femininity. Eventually turning back the way they had come, he was astounded at how difficult it was to ride away from

Anna-Maria Crogan.

As he headed back towards Casa Grande he told himself that it had been a mistake to follow her out of town. Yet, though he doubtless would have cause to regret it in the future, right then it was a mistake that he was pleased to have made.

The town was in the grip of the deep silence of night as he rode through a deserted main street to Jimpy Caan's place. Tending to his horse, he then strolled leisurely to the hotel. Along the way he sensed that someone stood concealed in the shadows of a building's overhang, watching him.

An automatic system of deduction in his nervous system came into play to identify the observer. Latigo called softly. 'Good night, Marshal.'

There was no reply.

★   ★   ★

Though Barry Cleat was still weak from loss of blood, his condition the following morning had a delighted Dr Hendly make the prognosis of a complete recovery. Coming out into the store, the pleased doctor gave Verity and her brother the good news. 'He's able to sit up and take notice.'

'Does Anna-Maria know that I've been shot?' Cleat later asked Verity.

'Yes,' she nodded. With Henry she had opened the store and then returned to their living quarters to make Cleat a light breakfast. 'She was here last night when they brought you in. Anna-Maria intended to stay beside you all night, but Doc Hendly and Marshal Steiner said she should return home otherwise her father would make trouble.'

'She is a fine woman,' Cleat said, plainly warmed by hearing that Anna-Maria wanted to watch over him through the night. 'I remember the stranger, Latigo, helping me, but can recall nothing after that, Verity. Was there any more shooting?'

Verity hesitated, wondering how much she should tell a man who was still so poorly. Accepting that he would soon learn what had taken place anyway, she explained. 'There was, Mr Cleat. Latigo killed the man who had shot you, and another man who was with him.'

'Who were there?' Cleat enquired, so shaken that Verity was sure that his face would have whitened had it not already been ashen.

'Two of Mr Crogan's men, Zeke Wiseman and Luke Rodgers.'

Aghast, Cleat said hoarsely, 'His two best guns. Crogan will be streaked.' A sudden thought had him ask urgently, 'Does Crogan know that I'm here, Verity?'

'I don't think so.'

'He'll soon find out, and make trouble for you and Henry. I'll move back to my place later today.'

'You won't be fit enough to do that for a week or so, Mr Cleat,' Verity protested. 'You just get yourself better. Don't worry about Henry and me.'

* * *

A dull headache made Brett Steiner irritable. Disturbed by the violent change in Casa Grande since Latigo had ridden in, the Marshal had slept little. Anxious over the possibility that Latigo had caused yet more trouble by following Anna-Maria, he had remained out in the street to be certain that Latigo came back into town. It hadn't been possible to stay hidden, and he was worried by the fact that Latigo had known he was watching him. Things were moving fast. Too fast. The time was surely and swiftly approaching when he would be forced to take sides. If, as was likely, circumstances forced him to stand with Crogan, a man with Latigo's acute awareness and hair-trigger reflexes would be a dangerous foe.

It was concern about Latigo that had him sitting in the LC ranch house in late morning, listening to Crogan complain in a droning monotone.

'That's three good men I've lost in two days. You know what to do.'

'Either Wiseman or Rodgers shot Barry Cleat in the back last night,' Steiner said.

'I heard about that. Hurt bad, ain't he, Brett? Good thing. That fella's been making a play for Anna-Maria.'

'If Latigo hadn't got your boys I'd have locked them up for shooting Cleat, Lonroy.'

'You sure have got your loyalties twisted of late, Marshal. It's Latigo I want you to take care of.'

Rejecting this with a shake of his head, Steiner explained. 'Wiseman and Rodgers tried to drygulch Latigo, and he got the better of them. There's no crime for me to deal with.'

Sitting forward in his chair, Crogan jabbed a finger in Steiner's direction. 'He was here last night, Brett.'

'Who was?'

'Latigo.'

'He may be a fast gun, Lonroy, but Latigo's nobody's fool.'

'Maybe so, maybe not,' Crogan reasoned. 'But Anna-Maria's horse went lame last night, and someone brought her back. Braithwaite was on duty at the gate at the time. He saw Latigo in town the night he killed Clements, and he swears that it was him rode up with my daughter.'

'What does Anna-Maria say?'

'I haven't had the chance to ask her. I haven't even seen her this morning. She's still up in her room. She's a law unto herself, that one, Brett. What's with this Latigo? What is he? What's he after?'

'No more than a gambler looking for a big win, as far as I know,' the marshal replied. 'In the short time he's been in Casa Grande he's become a wealthy man.'

'When he should have been locked up from the minute he drew on Rube Clements. It's time for you to get down off that fence you've been sitting on, Brett,' Crogan retorted. 'No one kills three of my men and gets away with it. What are you going to do about this Latigo?'

'Unless he breaks the law, nothing.'

'That ain't good enough, Marshal,' Crogan protested menacingly. 'You can goad him, provoke him into slapping leather. That will be the end of it.'

'It's likely to be the end of me, Lonroy,' Steiner wasn't ashamed to admit. 'Then you wouldn't have anyone to take care of you now that you've lost Zeke and Luke.'

'Don't you be too certain of that, Brett,' Crogan cautioned. 'I'll be making some arrangements real soon, don't you worry.'

Hearing what Crogan had just said, and the way he said it, Brett Steiner was worried.

★　★　★

The dilapidated Kickapoo Saloon stood largely unnoticed and unpatronized at the far end of the main street from the Lazy Horse Saloon. Though it was close to noon when Latigo entered the place, the interior was dark and gloomy. Jimpy

Caan had warned him that the saloon had been neglected, but that hadn't prepared Latigo for the scene that confronted him. Everything about the saloon was uninviting. Though open for business, there was not one customer present. According to Jimpy, competition from the Lazy Horse had virtually put the Kickapoo out of business and brought the owner, Rick Colbourn to the verge of financial ruin. Lonroy Crogan, Jimpy reported, was hovering like a vulture, ready to swoop in and add the saloon to his business empire.

Jimpy sang the praises of Rick Colbourne, who had arrived in Casa Grande with his wife in a wagon selling Kickapoo Snake Oil and other elixirs. Though the concoctions he peddled were dubious at least, and worthless at most, the elegantly attired Colbourn had a flair for business that earned him enough to buy and rename what was then the Treble Chance Saloon.

'What can I get you, stranger?'

Latigo's eyes had not yet adjusted

from coming in out of the sunlight. It seemed to him that a man had appeared behind the bar as if by magic. He was a stocky, balding man who gave Latigo a half smile because the right side of his face didn't participate. His cheek remained still, a slight drooping to it that was most noticeable in the way that the side of his mouth was dragged down. Seeing the semi-lifeless face brought to mind Jimpy's story of how Colbourne had once made his saloon attractive by installing a stage and putting on new shows with a different theme every week. African, Egyptian, French and English, the shows had been highly popular. Business at the Lazy Horse had suffered severely as a consequence.

One night when the Kickapoo was packed to capacity, Crogan had sent men to infiltrate the crowd and start a riot. Many of the customers had been badly injured, the entertainers had been terrified to the extent that no artistes were ever again prepared to work at the saloon, and Rick Colbourne had been beaten to within an inch of his life. The nerves in the right side of his face had not recovered, and never would.

'A bottle of rye,' Latigo ordered. 'And I'd be obliged if you'd bring it to that table in the corner and join me.'

Made suspicious by the invitation, Colbourne asked, 'Why would you want me to drink with you?'

'I'd like to talk business.'

With an indifferent shrug, Colbourne turned away to reach for a bottle and two glasses. By the time Latigo had walked to the table and was sitting down, the saloon owner was pulling out the chair opposite to him.

Latigo introduced himself. 'My name is Abel Latigo.'

'Rick Colbourne. I'd be lying if I said I hadn't heard of you.' Though only in early middle age, something important had already died in Colbourne's eyes.

They shook hands, and then Latigo looked around him as he poured them both a drink. He remarked superfluously, 'Business isn't good.'

'It couldn't be worse,' Colbourne said. 'I came to Casa Grande with a dream and money nine years ago. Now I spend every minute of every day wondering what happened to both my dream and the money. I stand in an empty saloon awaiting the inevitable.'

'Which is?'

'Selling out to Crogan for a pittance.'

Colbourne looked in need of another drink. Latigo poured him one, saying, 'It doesn't have to be that way.'

'What other way can there be?' Colbourne enquired in a despairing tone.

'Sell the place to me. I'll pay you a fair price. Enough to settle any problems you might have, with some spare for a new start.'

For a fleeting second Colbourne's eyes came alive with hope, then worry clouded them over. 'There can be no new start. I have a sick wife upstairs, Latigo. The longer I hang on here, the

127

longer I keep a roof over our heads.'

'That's no problem,' Latigo responded. 'You sell to me, and I'll keep you on to run the saloon. I will put money into the place, put the Kickapoo on a sure footing.'

'Why would you be prepared to do that?' Colbourne questioned, almost jubilant but afraid to believe what he had just heard.

'I have my reasons.'

Colbourne shook his head doubtfully. 'No, that would be to exchange one hopeless dream for another hopeless dream. If I sell out to you, Crogan would get me. What would happen to my wife then?'

'I'll take care of Crogan. He won't harm either your wife or you.'

'That's a mighty big boast that tells me you don't know Crogan,' Colbourne argued.

'I know Lonroy Crogan better than anyone here in Casa Grande does,' Latigo said, quietly and evenly. 'I'll give you until tomorrow morning, Colbourne. If

I drop by then and you say no, then that will be that. Should you decide to take up my offer, then we'll go to the bank and get everything settled.'

★   ★   ★

'Where are you going?'

'I'm riding into town,' Anna-Maria stiffly answered her father's question. Delaying facing him that morning had made it more difficult when she had forced herself to do so. 'I'm worried about him.'

'Why?' Crogan frowned.

How could she respond to that question? Had anyone else asked it would have been suffice to reply that Cleat was a human being. But that was something her father would be unable to grasp. That he obviously loved her very deeply yet possessed little or no feeling for anyone else had puzzled Anna-Maria for as long as she could remember.

'We Crogans have a status to

maintain, Anna-Maria,' her father told her forcefully. 'There will be a lot of talk in Casa Grande when people see you calling at Doc Hendly's to enquire after Cleat.'

'Barry isn't at the doctor's home. He's at Henry and Verity Whitsall's place.'

Though he tried to conceal it, she could read in her father's face the effect this information had on him. He was patently pleased to learn the whereabouts of Barry Cleat. That didn't bode well for Cleat or the Whitsalls, and she felt guilty about having spoken without thinking. Guilty and very afraid.

Covering his interest in what he had just learned, he warned her, 'No good can come from mixing too much with these people, Anna-Maria. I've got a business to run, a business that one day will be yours, and the Barry Cleats of this world have no part to play in that.'

Anna-Maria detested the arrogance of his remark, while at the same time recognizing that it was the sort of thing that she said, the kind of thoughts that she had, though not where Barry Cleat was concerned, but about the majority of the people of the area. She found this involuntary self-assessment to be painful.

Aware that it would be futile to argue, Anna-Maria changed the subject to her horse. 'I must go to have Dalton fix Caesar's shoe.'

'I had him do that first thing this morning.'

'Thank you, father,' Anna-Maria said quickly as she hurried out of the door to avoid him telling her in his stentorian voice that if she went into town it would be against his wishes.

Although her father always insisted that the hired hands were paid to carry out duties such as saddling her horse, Anna-Maria, as always, saddled Caesar herself. This put the cowboys watching her in a dilemma. They were too frightened of her to intervene, and terrified of her father because they hadn't insisted on helping her.

Mounting up, she mockingly gave the hands what was a cross between a wave and a salute, reined the stallion round, and rode away.

Reaching the edge of town she saw Latigo coming out of the Kickapoo. Seeing him reminded her that he had been often in her thoughts since leaving her at the LC Ranch entrance last night. Concern about her father's reaction to her intended visit to the injured Barry Cleat had forced Latigo from her mind. But now, after having seen herself clearly a little earlier, she was perturbed by the thought of what impression of her he had gained last night. This brought another realization to her; that she wouldn't care about that had it been any man but Latigo.

Tempted now to rein her horse over to speak to him, she resisted the urge. Maybe she didn't share her father's notion that he was the feudal lord of the territory and she was some kind of a princess, but Anna-Maria was too full of pride even to cross the street to speak to a stranger, a drifter, who plainly considered himself as her equal.

Even so, as she rode on up the street at a steady pace, she found herself wondering if he had noticed her. Latigo was something more than a cut above the range-drifters that occasionally arrived at the LC Ranch seeking temporary work. That he was a man with poise and impeccable manners, with a knowledge of plays and play-wrights, intrigued her.

Thoughts of Latigo were still plaguing her when she dismounted outside of the Whitsall store and hitched Caesar to the rail. Recall of how badly injured Barry Cleat had been had her prepare for the worst as she walked in the door. The smile Verity gave her chased most of her fears away.

'It's great news, Anna-Maria. Mr Cleat is recovering fast,' Verity announced. She suggested, 'Please go through. I know he is most anxious to see you.'

Anna-Maria hesitated. Henry smiled a greeting at her from where he was weighing out alfalfa, and she smiled back. Verity and her brother were two nice people, and she felt that she ought to warn them of her unintentional mistake in telling her father that they had taken Barry Cleat in. She paused to think it through. Though being vindictive was one of her father's many faults, she couldn't in any way be sure that he would make a move against the Whitsalls for harbouring one of his main business rivals.

She decided that she would be wrong to tell Verity and Henry. That would cause them constant worry about something that probably would never happen. Thanking Verity, and walking through the store to the living quarters, Anne-Maria was aware that she had just lied to herself so as to take the easy option.

6

The sun of a new day was still a few hours away from its zenith when Crogan stood beside his horse on a high hill. This was his favourite location. As a man who found it impossible to change his habits, he rode out here every morning. Even the close to threadbare chesterfield overcoat he had on, its velvet collar scuffed and holed, had been part of the daily ritual from the beginning. To stand here and look down on a vast sweep of grassland stretching to a far-distant horizon, knowing that he owned all that he could see, imparted a feeling more heady, more intoxicating, than anything he had ever experienced in his life. Being out here was the only time of the day that he was at ease without protection from his hired gunslingers. There was something holy about this hill. He was always aware of something unseen but powerful watching over him here.

Marginally spoiling the morning for him was his concern over Anna-Maria. His daughter had been all of the previous day in town, returning to the ranch a little before midnight. The only explanation could be that she had spent long hours with Barry Cleat at the Whitsall home. Crogan had three reasons for objecting to the burgeoning relationship between Anna-Maria and Cleat. They were that Cleat wasn't good enough for his daughter, that he was a business rival, and that the time would come when Crogan would use any means to put Cleat out of business. That would mean publicly destroying his son-in-law if what was between Cleat and his daughter should evolve into marriage.

Something down below caught his eye, distracting him. It was a rider. Now at the foot of the hill, the horseman had begun a steady ascent. Crogan's hour of spiritual communion with his wealth and power was ruined by an ice-cold fear that spread rapidly from the nape of his neck throughout his body to cause an unpleasant tingling sensation all over his scalp. His fervent belief in the godliness of the hill deserted him. A sense of vulnerability pushed his fear to the border of terror.

Then the diminutive horse and rider grew larger as they drew closer. A few minutes later, Lonroy Crogan breathed a throat-rattling sigh of relief as he recognized the approaching horseman as Ben Ringstead.

Yet the fear had gone only to be replaced by apprehension. It would take a serious matter to have the property dealer ride all the way out here from Casa Grande. Ringstead was strictly a town man with an aversion to the great outdoors. The gaming tables were his natural habitat. The expression on Ringstead's face as he rode up and dismounted justified Crogan's dread.

'What brings you all the way out

here, Ben?' he enquired, falteringly.

Ringstead delayed his reply while he used a kerchief to wipe a mortar of trail dust mixed with sweat from his face. A face so thin that the bones looked sharp enough to cut through the tightly stretched skin. Then he answered. 'Latigo had another big win last night.'

'Did you ride out here to tell me that, Benjamin?' an annoyed Crogan asked.

'When I say big, Lon, I mean *big*,' Ringstead emphasized.

'Your skill with the cards has always impressed me, Ben. Did you lose?'

'Very heavily,' Ringstead answered nervously. 'As did many others. Latigo is an exceptional gambler.'

'A card sharp,' Crogan said judgementally.

'There is nothing to suggest so. But the fact that he appears to be unbeatable presents a challenge that can't be ignored by inveterate gamblers.'

'People such as yourself.' Crogan uttered a criticism, his eyes hard and cold now as he looked out over his domain. He told Ringstead, 'Latigo's days are numbered. I have many powerful connections, and yesterday I laid the foundations for Latigo's downfall. Let's talk business now. Tell me, how are the Whitsall repayments fixed?'

'Better than they were. There are two months outstanding, but Henry has promised that he'll bring everything up to date today.'

Crogan had hoped for a worse report. By taking Cleat in and encouraging Anna-Maria in her fascination with the man, the Whitsalls had seriously stepped out of line. His slit of a wide mouth opened and closed like a trap when he spoke. 'That's not good enough, Benjamin.'

'I trust the Whitsalls, Lon,' Ringstead protested.

'That won't do,' Crogan said adamantly. 'Ride back in with me Ben, and I'll explain along the way.'

★ ★ ★

Gently sliding the deed across his desk towards Colbourn, Barton Travers jabbed a stubby finger at it, saying, 'Just sign there, Rick.'

Colbourne put his signature beside that of Latigo, then leaned back in his chair. 'That's it, Mr Travers. Latigo, I sure hope that you can back up your promise to me.'

'Let me put your mind at rest, Rick,' Travers smiled helpfully. 'In the short time Mr Latigo has been in town I have learned to trust him completely.'

The lifeless side of his face served to deepen Colbourne's worried expression. 'With respect, you are talking money, Mr Travers, whereas my problem is Lonroy Crogan and the roughnecks he employs.'

'You have my promise, Rick. Fix me up with a room at the Kickapoo and I'll check out of the hotel today,' Latigo spoke up before turning to Travers. 'I intend to refurbish the saloon, Barton. It has to be a quick job but a good job. Can you recommend anyone?'

'I certainly can,' Travers gave Latigo a

fat-lipped smile. 'Peter Graham is your man. He's the finest carpenter I have ever had the pleasure to witness at work.'

'He's sure had a lot of practice at woodwork since you came to town, Latigo,' Colbourne sardonically remarked.

Latigo grinned as he warned 'Take too many liberties and you'll find yourself out of work, Rick.'

'Finding myself with a Crogan bullet in my back is my worry,' Colbourne said half-jokingly as he and Latigo stood and shook hands in turn with Barton Travers.

'The best of luck in your new venture, Abel,' Travers said.

★   ★   ★

Casa Grande's main street was busy in early afternoon as Verity Whitsall made her way towards Benjamin Ringstead's office. In a pale blue Dolly Varden dress, and with her red hair held stylishly in a chignon, her appearance and prettiness diverted attention from her lame leg. There was a lot of money in the cloth bag that she carried under one arm. Hard-earned money that Verity hated to part with, but accepted that it was necessary. Her reluctance was eased by the fact that the last couple of days' trading had been far busier than usual. If things stayed that way, something she was frightened to hope for, Henry and she would be able to keep their heads above water, but still they would never achieve financial independence.

Alice Morrish, the Pastor's wife, spotted her from the other side of the street and came hurrying across to ask, 'How is Mr Cleat, Verity?'

'He's doing well, Alice, really well.'

'Thank the Lord,' the older woman said in relief. 'Pastor Morrish will be visiting him tonight, if that is convenient for you and your brother.'

Placing an affectionate hand on her friend's bony shoulder, Verity smilingly reassured her. 'Of course, the pastor will be most welcome. How is he after his frightening experience, Alice?'

'He's getting over it slowly, Verity. It's strange, as the pastor abhors violence, but he has nothing but admiration for this Mr Latigo. What is your opinion of him?'

'I've only met him briefly,' Verity answered, wondering if she should voice what she felt about the stranger. 'To be honest, Alice, he frightens me terribly.'

With a wise nod, Alice Morrish commiserated. 'I can empathize, my dear. We are not accustomed to mixing with men such as he. We must pray that Mr Latigo takes his leave of our town before any further tragedies occur.'

Agreeing, though she was otherwise convinced, Verity said farewell to the pastor's wife and went on her way with the mysterious and disturbing Latigo very much on her mind. Verity was certain that Latigo had come to Casa Grande for a purpose. Whatever that purpose was, there would be a lot more trouble before he left. That filled her with dread, as Latigo had become a regular part of Henry's conversations with her. That morning she had found him sitting by Barry Cleat's bed talking, and the topic had been Abel Latigo. Verity's fear was that with Latigo for a hero, Henry would want to become proficient with a gun.

Ceasing her thoughts about Latigo and concentrating on the business at hand, she opened the door of Ringstead's office and walked in. The property dealer and moneylender was standing studying a map pinned to the wall. When he turned to face her she suspected that something was wrong. Though Ringstead's politeness never edged into anything resembling friendliness, right then he was made even more distant by what Verity judged to be embarrassment.

'There we are, Mr Ringstead, right up to date,' she said more cheerfully than she felt, as she emptied the money out of her bag on to his desk.

Not responding, Ringstead walked behind his desk. He tidied the money, putting the notes and coins into some sort of order. Assuming that he was about to start counting the money, Verity was surprised when he put a hand towards her and gestured that he wanted her bag. Nonplussed, she passed the bag to him, and he started putting the money back into it.

'Whatever is this, Mr Ringstead?' Verity worriedly enquired.

'I am sorry, Miss Whitsall,' Ringstead said, made sly by an inability to face her. 'A mountain of arrears on repayments has forced the introduction of a new policy.'

'But,' Verity argued weakly in a small voice, looking pensively out the window. 'The money I have here brings our account right up to the minute.'

'I appreciate that, Miss Whitsall, but I am afraid that I can't make exceptions. You will be the first to agree that your brother and yourself have not always toed the line, as it were, where repayments are concerned.'

'Things have been difficult, I admit that. But we have always made it. We have never kept you waiting overlong, Mr Ringstead.'

Even more uncomfortable than before, Ringstead told her, 'I have taken that into consideration, Miss Whitsall, but money is tight in the area right now. All of Casa Grande's businesses are beginning to feel the pinch, and I am afraid that you and your brother may find things more difficult in the very near future.'

'That isn't necessarily so,' Verity argued. 'What you predict may never happen, Mr Ringstead. Look, please take the money now and let us wait to see how things work out.'

'I am so sorry,' Ringstead said with a shake of his head. 'You are asking me to take a chance, a considerable gamble, with my money, Miss Whitsall.'

'But there is no alternative.'

He lowered his voice confidentially.

'There is. My advice is that you should sell up as soon as possible.'

'We could never find a buyer quickly,' Verity protested, her bottom lip trembling.

'I can help you there if you would permit me.'

The knowledge that he was about to suggest Crogan as a buyer, had Verity turn quickly and leave the office before Ringstead could see the useless tears brimming her eyes. Stepping out on to the boardwalk, Verity felt as if she had stepped into some strange world where all the things that governed what she knew had been suspended.

★ ★ ★

Learning from Barton Travers that Latigo had purchased the Kickapoo Saloon added more misery to what was already a bad day for Marshal Steiner. The news came shortly after he had discovered that Crogan had used his considerable influence to avenge the killing of Wiseman and Rodgers. The crafty Crogan was employing the law in his campaign against Latigo. This meant that Steiner would be caught in the middle, and he didn't like it. Crogan wasn't the kind of man to allow anyone to push him an inch, and there was nothing in the world that could divert Latigo from the vengeance mission he was on.

There was a widening rift between Crogan and the marshal that couldn't be detected mentally, yet Steiner could clearly sense it. He found it disquieting. For a long time he had profited from his association with Crogan without any serious compromising of his duties as a law officer. In the coming war between Crogan and Latigo, Steiner was likely to be the first casualty, figuratively speaking. To take control he would have to enforce the law. If that meant making an enemy of Crogan, as was most probable, the marshal would suffer a rude awakening from his cherished dream of a comfortable retirement.

Though regarding that as a personal tragedy, Steiner was aware that he had some kind of instinctive rapport with Latigo. Steiner attributed this to the younger man's superb confidence in his own reflexes and skill with a six-shooter reminding him of himself fifteen or so years ago.

Entering the Kickapoo, Steiner was met by the pleasant and unmistakable smell of freshly cut wood. With Latigo watching, Peter Graham was constructing what promised to be an attractively modern bar when it was finished. Rick Colbourne was busy sweeping up wood shavings and sawdust.

'You look like a man with a problem, Marshal,' Latigo remarked.

'I guess that you're right, Latigo, and I'm about to share it with you.' Steiner lit a cigar and waved the match around long after the flame had died. 'Lonroy Crogan has gone to the law over the deaths of Wiseman and Rodgers.'

Slowly placing the length of wood he was holding on the uncompleted bar,

Latigo enquired in a quiet voice, 'Have you come here to take me in, Steiner?'

'No.' Steiner looked as if he was about to say something more, then pressed his lips together.

'Then why are you here?'

Looking around him before replying, Steiner was astonished by the amount of work done in a short time. 'The coroner arrives in Casa Grande the day after tomorrow to hold an inquest on Wiseman and Rodgers. You'll have to be there, Latigo.'

'Will Crogan be there?'

'Nope,' Steiner answered, shrugging. 'He can afford to pay someone to represent him.'

'The coroner,' Latigo cynically suggested.

'You're probably right,' Steiner admitted. 'But when Crogan hears that you've bought this place, you would be wise to expect more trouble.'

'It's your job to protect me, Marshal,' Latigo said casually.

With a negative shake of his head,

Steiner denied this. 'I keep the peace, Latigo, by helping the abused and the innocent. Casa Grande doesn't pay me to rescue troublemakers from the trouble they cause.'

'Then I guess I'll have to handle it myself, Marshal.'

'That's mighty fine, providing that you keep within the law,' Steiner warned, adding as he walked away, 'Just be there at the inquest, Latigo.'

'I will,' Latigo promised.

★　★　★

In the cramped, melancholy room at the rear of the store, a white-faced, red-eyed Verity Whitsall felt like a small child confiding an illogical nightmare. A silent and solemn Pastor Morrish listened, while her brother sat miserably, holding his head in his hands. Henry's bedroom door was open and Barry Cleat, propped up into a sitting position in bed, un-happily observed the little drama being played out in the other room.

'If I had the money to help you in this situation, Verity,' the pastor said, 'I wouldn't hesitate. I am very aware of the effort you have put into, and the love that you have for this store.'

'I know that you would help us, Pastor Morrish,' Verity assured him, reaching out to cover one of his hands with hers and give it a gentle squeeze.

'I could find some paid work while you look after the shop, Verity,' Henry suggested.

Looking lovingly at her brother, Verity told him, 'That wouldn't be enough, Henry.'

'Verity's right,' Barry Cleat unexpectedly spoke up from the bedroom. 'I appreciate that this is a family matter, but no amount of money would be enough.'

'Why do you say that, my good sir?' Pastor Morrish questioned. 'I was considering that members of my congregation might be prepared to invest in the business.'

'That wouldn't work, Pastor. I don't

doubt that I will be the next one that Crogan puts pressure on, and I have accepted defeat in advance,' Cleat admitted.

Sucking air deep into her lungs in a reverse sigh, Verity asked, 'Is there nothing we can do?'

'Nothing,' Cleat advised flatly, but with much sympathy.

'Whatever you say, I don't intend to let it happen,' Henry hotly declared.

'I believe that what Mr Cleat said is correct, son,' Pastor Morrish told Henry. 'It would be in the best interests of your sister and yourself if you bowed to the inescapable.'

Verity's worries and fears were increased tenfold when she noticed that her brother's manner revealed that he was not prepared to accept Pastor Morrish's advice.

★ ★ ★

Used as the venue for the inquest, the theatre was crowded. Sitting in line against one wall were four men whom Latigo had not seen before, but who were evidently the coroner's jury. The gap between the jury and the front row of seats was the only vacant space in the building. Seated together at one end of the front row were Henry and Verity Whitsall, together with Pastor Morrish. In one corner Marshal Steiner was holding a serious conference with Barton Travers. Anna-Maria Crogan sat like an ancient high priestess, straight-backed, alone and isolated, in a chair against a side wall.

She and Latigo had arrived simultaneously outside of the theatre. Passing him by, she had then halted and taken two steps back to stand facing him. Her grey eyes had returned his gaze with a wary unfriendliness. 'It wouldn't do for me to be seen talking to the enemy.'

'I hadn't realized that I was the enemy,' Latigo had replied.

She had gestured at the door of the theatre with a sideways tilt of her head. 'The show my father is putting on in there is for your benefit.'

'I kinda gathered that. But that doesn't prevent you and me from being friends.'

Lowering her head in thought, she had then looked up at him. 'Perhaps not. I wouldn't like to go in there with you feeling animosity towards me.'

'Then we are friends,' Latigo had said. 'Shake on it?'

They shook hands solemnly, staring at each other. Latigo had been perturbed by the look in Anna-Maria's eyes. Then she had gone.

Now the coroner, an unremarkable little man who had the look of someone who wished he were somewhere else, spoke to Marshal Steiner, who faced the assembly.

'Coroner Laslo is ready to start this inquiry,' Steiner announced.

Laslo frowned indecisively as he addressed the jury. 'Gentlemen, you have already been sworn in as a jury. We are here to investigate the recent demise of one Zeke Wiseman and one Luke

Rodgers. I now call Town Marshal Steiner to relate to the jury how he came upon the bodies of the two deceased.'

As Steiner faced the coroner, Latigo recognized the difficult position the marshal was in. Undoubtedly both the coroner and his jury had been chosen by Crogan to reach a verdict that Wiseman and Rodgers had been killed unlawfully. A verdict that would oblige Steiner to arrest Latigo immediately for murder. Not being present at the shooting gave the marshal room for manoeuvre when giving his evidence. Even so, he was in no position to oppose the verdict that Crogan wanted.

'I first discovered the body of Rodgers,' Steiner began. 'The force of a rifle bullet had sent the body through the glass window of a barber shop.'

'Force you say,' Laslo broke in importantly. 'Did you deduce from this that the rifle had been fired at a close range?'

'Yes. The man who had fired the shot

was at the scene holding a rifle.'

'Is that man here at this meeting, Marshal Steiner?'

Steiner turned to look directly at Latigo. 'He is. That is the man, Abel Latigo.'

'Did he own the rifle?'

'No, the rifle belonged to Wiseman, who was already dead at the time, having been shot in the church across the street.'

'I see.' Laslo showed his disgust on hearing of such lawlessness. 'So Wiseman had been shot and his rifle taken from him.'

'The shot that killed Wiseman had come from his own rifle,' Steiner corrected the coroner.

'From what we have heard, gentlemen,' Laslo turned to the jury. 'There can be only one verdict, and that is that both the deceased were murdered.'

There was a disturbance in the seated gathering as Henry Whitsall struggled to get to his feet while his sister attempted to hold him down.

Freeing himself of Verity's clutching hands, Henry shouted at the coroner, 'Pastor Morrish witnessed both shootings. In the interest of justice he must be permitted to testify.'

'Sit down, young man,' Laslo roared. 'This is an official inquiry and you are out of order.'

There was absolute silence in the building as Henry stayed defiantly on his feet. Everyone waited, wondering how the stand-off would end. It was Marshal Steiner who took Coroner Laslo by surprise by speaking up.

'The boy is right. Pastor Morrish can give this inquiry an exact account of what happened that night.'

'I would suggest, Marshal Steiner, that you are exceeding your duty,' Laslo rebuked Steiner.

Keenly interested in the outcome of the confrontation, Latigo waited to discover which way Steiner would go. It was make or break time for the marshal. To continue opposing Laslo might not have Steiner totally alienate Lonroy Crogan, but it would certainly incur his wrath.

'I disagree,' Steiner faced Laslo squarely. 'I have a duty to uphold the law here in Casa Grande, and in this instance the law demands by any interpretation that Pastor Morrish is allowed to testify.'

A ripple of support from the assembly was gaining volume when the coroner conceded defeat with a curt nod.

'Please be silent now,' Steiner told the crowd, then pointed a finger at Morrish. 'Please stand, Pastor, and tell the jury exactly what happened on the night Wiseman and Rodgers were shot.'

Henry Whitsall sat as Pastor Morrish stood and began hesitantly to relate the details of the shooting. He had a presence that was immediately reassuring. A hushed assembly eagerly waited to hear what he had to say. Gaining confidence, he testified that one of the two dead men had shot Barry Cleat, an innocent bystander, in the back. Then he went on to describe the situation at the church, where Wiseman had concealed himself in the belltower with the intention of shooting Latigo as he came down the street.

'That was Casa Grande's darkest night,' the clergyman said. 'Here today we are pointlessly inquiring into how two foul murderers came to die. I will tell you how in just one short sentence, Coroner Laslo. It was the Lord's swift and just retribution.'

Pastor Morrish was applauded by all those seated around him and the uproar continued until an angry Laslo, his face purple from shouting for the meeting to come to order, eventually regained order. Even so, the testimony of the clergyman had the coroner anguished.

Desperation had him try to regain control of the hearing by announcing, 'A coroner's inquest can't be closed until all the evidence is in.'

'We've heard all the evidence we need to hear,' a man shouted from the centre of the room.

There was a roar of support for this

from the gathering. With the majority of the people standing and leaving the building, the inquest ended in disarray and without a verdict returned by the jury.

7

With the refurbishment of the Kick-apoo Saloon proceeding at a fast pace, Latigo had employed Henry Whitsall in a part-time capacity as a painter and decorator. In addition to the extra money he was earning, Henry was filled with pride at being given the job by Latigo. The enigmatic stranger was to Henry the personification of all the legendary frontiersmen in his favourite dime novels. His sister saw working at the saloon as a reward for his intervention at the inquest, but Henry couldn't equate that mediocre incident with the kudos that came with a man such as Latigo regarding him as a person of worth.

In early evening, the saloon seemed very large due to him being all alone. Latigo was doing business of some kind at the bank, while Rick Colbourne was accompanying his wife on a visit to Doc Hendly. Henry was taking meticulous care in painting a long wall when four men entered. They stood together inside the door, looking around them. There was nothing unusual in this. Ever since Latigo had begun restoring the saloon there had been a fairly constant flow of short-term visits from the curious.

One of the four walked slowly over to stand by Henry and watch him at his work. The man was young, with long hair drooping like string from under his Stetson. His narrow face had the unmistakable cunning that comes from leading a decadent life, and his thin body was alert with the tension of a hunting animal. The fact that he stood there without uttering a word caused Henry unease.

The man at his side turned his head to grin at his companions. Then without any warning he kicked out at the stool on which Henry's large tin of paint stood. As the stool went flying, the paint tin upturned to splash paint over a wide area, ruining the completed furnishings near to where Henry had been working.

'Hey — ' Henry shouted angrily at the man.

Grinning at Henry, the man who had kicked the stool over made no move as the other three ruffians came over to join him. Then all four of them moved in threateningly on Henry.

★   ★   ★

'Good evening, Mr Latigo.'

Passing the bank as Latigo stepped out on to the boardwalk, Verity Whitsall had to summon up every ounce of her courage to utter the greeting. With Latigo having provided her brother with work at an unbelievably high rate of pay, she felt that she had to speak. Nevertheless, Latigo frightened her even more close up.

'Good evening to you, Miss Whitsall,' Latigo said with a smile that Verity

164

discovered was surprisingly pleasant. 'If you are on your way home I would be honoured to accompany you as far as the Kickapoo.'

'Most kind,' Verity managed to say.

She was very conscious of her lameness as they walked together. Put at her ease by Latigo's light conversation Verity discovered that she was enjoying his company. For the first time since her home and business had been put under threat, that worry wasn't taking precedence in her mind. It was impossible to regard the Latigo she was with as the infamous Latigo who had killed three men in less than three days. They neared the saloon sooner than she would have liked.

Latigo puzzled her by falling silent and slowing his steps when they were within a few feet of the Kickapoo. To Verity it seemed he could feel, practically almost taste, an increasingly potent danger in the atmosphere. Then she heard an agonized groan coming from within the saloon, and would have run to the door had not Latigo restrained her by holding her arm.

'Leave this to me, Miss Whitsall,' he said, speaking urgently. 'You go straight home.'

He left her then, moving fast to the open door of the Kickapoo and going in. Disobeying his instructions, Verity went up to the door and looked in. The scene inside had her recoil in horror with a hand to her mouth.

* * *

As the day drew to a close at a pleasant temperature, Anna-Maria and Lonroy Crogan sat on the veranda of the ranch house. Her father's manner bewildered Anna-Maria. Aware that he would have been brought news of the inconclusive end to the inquest long before she had reached home, she was surprised to find him unusually subdued. He seemed dispirited, although that was a state of mind she would never have associated with her father. This caused her to suffer a few pangs of guilt. Though she was quick to oppose him strongly whenever his strictness threatened her independence, she had never been disloyal. Yet the fact that the inquest had ended in Latigo's favour, while being a disaster for Lonroy Crogan, had her shamed by her earlier outrageously flirtatious encounter with Latigo. Not only had she let her father down, but also she had in a way betrayed the trusting and dependable Barry Cleat.

She had to admit, however, that she was attracted to Latigo. Anna-Maria had failed to convince herself that this attraction was due solely to Latigo being a newcomer to the district. Conscious that it was much more than that, she couldn't define what it was.

Her father broke in on her thoughts by saying, 'It was a new experience for me.'

'What was, father?' Anna-Maria enquired, although she already knew the answer.

'The inquest, g'hal,' he replied

calmly. 'It was a direct challenge to my authority such as I am not accustomed to.'

His use of g'hal, meaning tomboy, his pet name for her when she had been younger, warmed Anna-Maria. Sipping a glass of wine, enjoying the rare father and daughter intimacy of that early evening, she commented, 'I am certain that it won't take you long to recover from it, father.'

'Revenge is sweet,' he said with one of his odd smiles that went inwards for his personal enjoyment.

Anna-Maria didn't ask what form his revenge would take or, more likely, was taking right then. She preferred not to know, so complimented him instead. 'I have never known anyone to get the better of Lonroy Crogan.'

'And no one ever will,' he stated without the profound belief that was so characteristic of him. 'But there is an aspect to what has been happening of late that I am unable to fathom.'

'That is unlike you, father.'

'It is, and that concerns me greatly, Anna-Maria. At times like this I miss the army, where I had absolute control. Every situation then had an absolute certainty about it. Is it coincidence that a stranger rides into Casa Grande, and every move he makes since arriving directly affects me?'

'How could it be anything else?'

Crogan appeared to do a mental shaking of his head in wonderment. 'That's the question I have been asking myself. Is he just up to some shecoonery in general, or is it aimed at me?'

'Do you know, or know of, anyone named Latigo?'

'I've run that question through my mind continuously,' Crogan answered. 'The name means absolutely nothing to me.'

'There you are then, father. All that has happened has to be coincidence.'

'For some odd reason I am unable to give credence to that, Anna-Maria.'

The way her father said this shocked Anna-Maria. He was actually showing something edging on fear. He recovered rapidly, but having glimpsed what she had always regarded as an omnipotent god suddenly become impotent, no matter how briefly, unnerved her. For the first time she felt sorry for her father.

*   *   *

Verity's brother, beaten and bloodied, lay on the floor of the saloon surrounded by four men. One of the four, a lean man with long stringy hair, had one leg raised, about to kick Henry. Verity released a silent scream before realizing that the men were unaware of Latigo's arrival. He ran forwards and snaked out a foot to catch the back of the knee of the man standing on one leg. His leg going out from underneath him, the man toppled backwards, but Latigo acted while the ruffian's shoulders were still some four feet from the floor. He kicked out again, the flat of his booted right foot slamming into the back of the man's head and neck. Impelled by the force of the kick, the man hurtled to smash hard against the wall that Henry had freshly painted. As he slid down to a heap on the floor, his broken face was a grotesque blend of bright red blood and green wet paint.

Then Verity tried to shout a warning as one of the other men swung a right-hand punch at Latigo. But, perfectly balanced on the balls of his feet, Latigo easily ducked under the arm and drove home two hard punches, a left and a right, to the man's stomach. As the man was doubled over by the terrific blows, Latigo swung an arm to hit him hard on the back of the neck so that his face smashed into a table to the cracking, creaking sounds of bones breaking and gristle giving way.

But Latigo was then in serious trouble. One of the remaining two men had picked up a heavy chair, which he swung to crack Latigo hard on the back of the head. Felled by the blow, Latigo hit the floor face down and unconscious. Wasting no time in taking advantage of this, the fourth man jumped with both feet off the ground. His intention was to stomp on Latigo, but Verity breathed a sigh of relief as Latigo rolled to one side and the man's feet came heavily down on bare floorboards.

But Latigo had gained only a brief respite. Lying on his back now, still stunned, he was pinned to the floor by the man who had hit him with the chair, who now placed a booted foot on his throat. With a wide grin that was an ugly grimace on his face, the fourth man got ready to stomp on the body of a helpless Latigo.

Unable to watch what was about to happen, Verity was turning her head away when she saw the inactive body of her brother stir slowly back into life. Though thankful that Henry wasn't dead, she was terrified by the thought of him regaining consciousness and joining in the violence that was going on around him.

Holding her breath, she watched Henry's eyes flicker open to take in the scene. Then his right hand moved a little, the movement gaining momentum as it edged towards a stool that lay on its side close to him.

As the fourth man bent his knees in preparation for jumping on Latigo, Henry's fingers closed round a leg of the stool. Moving his body on its side, he flung the stool at the man who had Latigo immobilized. The heavy seat of the stool collided with the side of the man's head. Knocked sideways, the man tried but failed to keep his balance. He crashed face first to the floor, while the freed Latigo rolled sideways and came agilely up on to his feet.

The fourth man abandoned his planned leap and turned to check if Henry presented any danger to him. He paid dearly for that brief distraction. Coming at him fast, Latigo used the heel of his right hand to slam a chopping blow across the man's throat.

Choking and gasping, he staggered back, but Latigo showed no mercy. Reaching with both hands to grasp the man's hair, Latigo yanked the man's head forwards while driving the higher part of his own forehead twistingly into the man's face.

Blood spurting from a wrecked nose and mouth, falling when Latigo released his hold on his hair, the man dropped to the floor where he lay gagging on his own blood. It was then that absolute raw terror had Verity find her voice at last as she noticed the man Henry had knocked unconscious covertly moving where he lay on the floor. He was reaching for a handgun that had been concealed about his person.

'Look out, Mr Latigo,' Verity screamed.

Instantly taking in what was happening, Latigo's right hand went down for a fast draw. But the holster was empty. His gun had fallen out during the fighting. Adjusting speedily, his left hand moved swiftly to the holster tied to his left leg, only to discover that the

174

gun was missing from that holster, too.

Though his movements were shaky, the man on the floor was encouraged by the knowledge that Latigo was unarmed. Gradually bringing up his six-shooter he held it with both hands as he aimed it at Latigo.

Crouching and weaving to make himself less of a target, Latigo dashed to pick up a heavy table. Taking three quick steps to stand over the man who now had the gun pointed at him, Latigo lifted the table high above his head. It seemed to Verity that everything happened simultaneously right then. Latigo threw the table down and there was the roar as the gun was fired. But everything else faded into insignificance then as the edge of the weighty table came down on the man's back, snapping his spine. The man's piercing screams had Verity clap her hands tightly over her ears.

At last the man's screams died away; the gurgling that came at the end of them was a sure sign that he was mortally injured. Verity opened her eyes to see post-death convulsions cause the two halves of the broken body writhe horribly, as separately as if they had been severed. Seeing that Latigo was standing unharmed, Verity ran into the saloon and knelt to take her brother in her arms.

Coming over to them, Latigo gently tilted Henry's head back and looked into his eyes before telling Verity, 'He will be fine, Miss Whitsall. I'll just clear up here and we'll get him home.'

'We should take him to Doc Hendly, Mr Latigo.'

'There's no need,' Latigo assured her as he walked to pick up his guns and quickly examine the weapons before reholstering them.

Going to the nearest of the unconscious men then, Latigo took hold of him with one hand on his belt and the other on his collar. Latigo dragged him across the floor and threw him out of the door into the street. Repeating this action with the other two men, he then walked to the dead man. Standing silently looking down at the body for a short period, Latigo then dragged it to the door and tossed it out on top of the other three.

When Latigo returned to the Whitsalls, Henry, though groggy, was shakily able to gain his feet. Taking one of his wrists, Latigo placed it over his own shoulder to support the youngster. He said, 'Let's get you home, Henry. You're the hero who saved my life.'

Hearing this, Henry managed painfully to arrange his swollen face into the semblance of a smile as, with support from Latigo and Verity, he was able to make it to the door of the saloon. The three of them stepped outside to see Rick and Greta Colbourne coming towards them, both of them terribly shocked to see the state that Henry was in, and the four men lying in the dust of the street.

'Crogan's men,' Latigo explained curtly. 'Get your wife safely inside, Rick, then go find Marshal Steiner to have him take care of them.'

'Special delivery,' Jimpy Caan announced cheekily as he drove the buckboard up to the LC ranch house. Marshal Steiner sat beside him on the high seat.

A frowning Lonroy Crogan and two of his hired guns approached the buckboard. Expecting Crogan's frown to change to an expression of rage as he saw the three men who lay bound hand and foot in the buckboard, a surprised Steiner watched the rancher's face grow pale. A state of anxiety wasn't a reaction he had ever expected to witness in Crogan. Turning on the buckboard's high seat, the marshal slipped a knife from its sheath and reached down to slash through the trio's bondage, freeing them.

Stirring stiffly, seriously disfigured and physically hampered by the damage inflicted on them by Latigo, the three men welcomed being helped down from the wagon by their two colleagues.

A stricken Crogan watched them in their pain, then looked up at Steiner.

'Where is Bob Haller?'

It was Jimpy Caan who answered. 'Haller's dead as a can of corned beef.'

'What happened to him, Brett?' Crogan enquired.

An eager Jimpy Caan answered the question. 'Haller made the mistake of tangling with Abel Latigo.'

'And Latigo shot him,' Crogan assumed in a despairing whisper.

Steiner corrected him. 'It wasn't like that, Lon. Haller tried to pull a gun on Latigo when he was unarmed.'

'And got his spine snapped like a carrot,' Caan added gleefully.

'This is getting out of hand, Marshal,' Crogan complained. He added sarcastically, 'Just as before, I suppose no one is to blame?'

'Not this time, Lon,' Steiner replied. Crogan appeared to have aged several years since the last time he had seen him. 'I reckon as how you have to take the blame. It was you who sent four border ruffians into town to rough up the Whitsall kid, and they got more than they bargained for.'

'This is an important question, Marshal, to which I expect a straight-forward answer,' Crogan said. 'Will there come a time when you will apprehend this renegade Latigo?'

'As I said before, Lon. If and when he breaks the law,' Steiner responded in his cool, detached way.

With a long, unwavering look at the marshal, Crogan queried, 'Whosoever Latigo might be, Brett, I cannot permit him to continue in this way. What if I have to break the law to stop him?'

A long silence followed in which not only Crogan but also everyone there awaited Marshal Steiner's answer. Holding Crogan's gaze steadily, Steiner then looked away and gave Cam an order. 'Take me back to town, Jimpy.'

As the buckboard rumbled off, Lonroy Crogan stood motionless, watching it until in the far distance a bend in the trail snatched the wagon from his sight. Only then did he turn and make his slow way back to the house.

* * *

Deep in thought, Latigo made his way down the main street neither noticing a build-up of cloud that was darkening the morning sun, nor the people around him. The previous evening he had helped Verity with her brother, taking him home and tending to his injuries. Before Latigo had left the Whitsall home, Barry Cleat had beckoned to him and related in a whisper the dire financial situation that Verity and Henry were in.

Later in the evening, after he had been made richer still by another game of poker, Latigo had broached the subject of the Whitsalls to Barton Travers. He had asked, 'What if I back Verity and Henry financially, Barton?'

'It would make no difference, Abel,' had been the banker's gloomy advice.

'Crogan wants to add their store to his empire, and that is that. Those kids don't have a chance. They hastened their own doom by sheltering Cleat.'

The injustice of this had Latigo persist. 'There has to be a way.'

'Let me sleep on it. Call at the bank in the morning, Abel,' Travers had said.

That was where Latigo was heading right then, when Anna-Maria Crogan came riding slowly up the street. Pulling on the reins of her horse when she reached Latigo, she dismounted and stepped up on the boardwalk. She stood facing him, her folded arms were brown-skinned and bare. Maturity had etched character into her face without affecting its attractiveness.

'I've heard about Henry Whitsall. How is he?' she asked. She appeared to be restrained, no longer so conscious of her position of privilege. Having pushed off her Stetson so that it rested on her upper back, she fiddled nervously with cord at her throat.

'He isn't badly hurt.'

'Because you saved him, the story goes,' she said. 'And Barry Cleat? Is he still on the mend?'

Latigo nodded. 'He is. I know that he would like to see you, so why don't you call in at the Whitsall store?'

'How can I?' She wasn't the self-assured, close to arrogant Anna-Maria that Latigo had met on the day of the inquest. 'I am out of excuses for the actions of my father. I need to talk to you.'

'You are talking to me now, Anna-Maria.'

'This can be seen as no more than the two of us passing the time of day.' She was covertly, but not slyly, watching Latigo's face carefully. 'My every move in town is reported to my father. There are some things that I would like to speak to you about.'

'Are they important?' Latigo warily asked. His intentions regarding Crogan prohibited even a mild friendship with his daughter.

'I believe so. Do you know Absaroka Peak?'

'I don't.'

'It's about five miles out of town,' she said, adding confidently, 'Jimpy Caan can give you directions. Could you meet me out there this afternoon?'

'Is this a good idea, Anna-Maria?'

'Probably not,' she frankly admitted. 'But I think it's essential that we do talk.'

She was going back to her horse when, as an afterthought, she said, 'Do I call you Abel?'

'That's fine with me.'

'Right, Abel. Until this afternoon at Absaroka Peak,' she said over her shoulder as she swung up into the saddle and rode away.

Unsure of what had just taken place, and what he had let himself in for by not refusing Anna-Marie's request that they meet, Latigo was aware of Brett Steiner standing in the doorway of the marshal's office across the street. Walking on, Latigo raised a hand to acknowledge Steiner's presence. He got no more than a curt nod in return.

At the bank, Barton Travers was as polite as ever but unenthusiastic in the extreme. 'I've given the Whitsall business a lot of thought, Abel, and have come up with the only possible solution. You buy the store and keep Verity and Henry on to run it, just as you did with the Kickapoo Saloon and Rick Colbourne.'

Latigo voiced his misgivings. 'That would mean me paying off their loan in full to Ben Ringstead, and Lon Crogan would never agree to that.'

'He wouldn't,' Travers concurred. 'But there is another way. I can arrange the paperwork for you to purchase the store direct from the Whitsalls, then you can pay off what they owe Ringstead through the bank.'

'That's fine with me, Barton, as I want to get Crogan riled up,' Latigo said. 'But by helping me you will be making an enemy of Crogan, too.'

That Travers was very aware of this was apparent by the way he dabbed at his sweating brow with a handkerchief.

He explained flatly, 'I am very mindful of that. But with Crogan now owning most of the town, it is only a matter of time before he takes over my bank. The avoidance of such empire building requires one to say nothing, do nothing, and therefore become nothing. So I've decided to make a stand right now.'

'You could regret doing so, Barton.'

'I might come to regret not doing so,' Travers countered.

'You're right,' Latigo conceded. 'You get the paperwork ready, Barton, and I'll put the idea across to Verity and Henry.'

★ ★ ★

A little way along the street from the bank, Latigo found a hostile Marshal Steiner waiting for him. 'I guess that I didn't have you figured right, Latigo.'

'How did you have me figured, Marshal?'

'Not as a man who would use a girl to get at her father,' Steiner replied.

'You were right the first time, Steiner,' Latigo said, controlling his anger. 'It's the other way around. The Crogan girl wants me to meet her for a talk out at Absaroka Peak, wherever that is.'

On hearing this, a confused Steiner cautioned, 'The peak is an ideal place for an ambush, Latigo.'

'I don't believe that Anna-Maria would set me up, not even for her father.'

'Neither do I,' the marshal said worriedly. 'But Lon Crogan is capable of pulling any stunt.'

'There's only one way to find out. How do I get to Absaroka Peak, Marshal?'

8

The wind was damp in Latigo's face as he moved into the foothills country four miles out of Casa Grande. Sure that Latigo would be riding into a trap, Steiner had reluctantly given him directions to Absaroka Peak. Though Latigo had become increasingly watchful, he didn't share the marshal's belief. Being the daughter of a wealthy man, the pretentious Anna-Maria compared badly in many ways to the down-to-earth saloon girls and frontier-women he was accustomed to. Yet he found it impossible to regard her as treacherous. His fear was that meeting her might well compromise his plan for vengeance against her father.

Ahead were the cliffs that Steiner had told him to look out for. The glare of the late afternoon sun was reflected in shining streaks above some straggling trees, enabling him to see the passage through the cliffs. Absaroka Peak lay just half a mile on from the end of the passage.

An instinct of self-preservation signalled an alarm to Latigo as he neared the entrance to the passage. Obeying the inner warning, he dismounted and looped the reins over the low limb of a pine. A thick carpet of wet needles muffled his footsteps as he moved through the pines into the passage. Robbed of sunlight by the high cliffs, Latigo pulled tight into a shallow fissure to study his surroundings. Remaining still he scanned the tops of the cliffs on both sides of the passage.

Satisfied after five uneventful minutes had passed, he was moving out of the fissure to head back to his horse, when he startled a bird that rose squawking up into the air. Immediately there came the echoing crack of a rifle from high up. A bullet chipped rock away close to Latigo's left side before noisily ricocheting.

Latigo reasoned that the man up on the cliff would have expected him to move to his right to go back to his horse. The fact that he had fired to Latigo's left indicated that he had a limited view of his hiding place. Putting his theory to the test, Latigo moved to the right out of the fissure. This brought a practically instantaneous bark of a rifle being fired, the bullet clipping rock away from the right of Latigo. Moving swiftly back in, Latigo knew that there were at least two men up on the cliff. The situation was even more dangerous than he had first thought. His handguns were made useless by distance.

The rumours about Town Marshal Steiner being on Crogan's payroll had proven to be true. Steiner must have sent a messenger to the LC Ranch with news of Latigo's intended meeting with Anna-Maria. His liking for the taciturn marshal made betrayal by him additionally hard for Latigo.

But indulging bitterness was no help. Crouching as low as possible, he would have to make a run for it back to the trees where he had tethered his horse. As a veteran gambler, Latigo was keenly aware that the odds were stacked heavily against him. Attempting to drop to a crouch before running he learned that the fissure was too shallow to permit such a move. A volley of rifle fire told him that he had revealed himself. Half blinded by the rock dust kicked up by bullets, he stood up straight and pulled his body tightly in. His situation was now so desperate that he could do nothing but wait until dark.

Pondering on this, Latigo thought he heard his name called, but blamed it on his imagination.

'Abel.'

This time there could be no mistake. The call had come from the trees. 'Abel. It's me, Jimpy Caan. Brett Steiner asked me to trail you in case you met trouble. I've got your rifle here.'

'What good is it to me there?' Latigo ungraciously asked, then regretted doing so.

'There's no call to be so goddam ornery, Abel,' an annoyed Jimpy called back. 'I'll force them two *hombres* up there to keep their heads down. Come a-running when I open fire.'

Steiner had sent Caan, which meant that the marshal hadn't tipped Crogan off. Latigo was struck by a sudden realization. Anna-Maria had set him up. He had no time to dwell on this as Caan started rapid rifle-fire. Leaping from the fissure, Latigo sprinted for the trees, arriving unscathed. Hunkering beside a tree reloading his rifle, Caan spoke without looking up. 'I reckons if we hit the trail and we'll be back in town afore candle-lighting time.'

'No,' Latigo said adamantly, certain that if he made it to Absaroka Peak Anna-Maria would be waiting for him there. She couldn't be a part of the treachery. 'You can head back to Casa Grande, Jimpy, but I'm going on to Absaroka Peak.'

'What happened to that nice, sensible Abel Latigo I met first just a few days ago?' Caan moaned. 'He sure has turned into a right ornery cuss. Has it slipped your mind that there's two rifles up there that don't want you to go nowhere?'

'I'm thinking on how to deal with them, Jimpy.'

'I've already thought,' Caan announced, throwing Latigo's rifle for him to catch. 'You take a regular shot at those guys with the rifles, just to have 'em think we're both down here.'

'What happened to your determination to ride back to town, Jimpy?' Latigo enquired.

'That was the white man part of me. Now you're going to see the Cherokee half take over. Probably you ain't noticed, but the cliffs on our side is higher than where them two are at. I'm going up high. Do the shooting I told you to do, and just wait for me to come back down.'

'What if you don't come back down, Jimpy?'

'Then don't waste your time by

coming to look for me, *mi amigo*,' Caan advised. Then he had gone.

Left alone, Latigo released an occasional shot at the clifftop, and received some desultory return fire. He hated to admit it but he couldn't bring himself to have faith in Caan, whose life seemed to revolve around the tragedy of losing a squaw wife to an Indian brave in the long distant past. Time passed slowly before he heard an exchange of fire that had him wait anxiously.

Then, without disturbing the pine needles underfoot, Caan came silently out of the trees to tell Latigo, 'Got 'em both, so now I'm riding back to town. It's safe for you to head on through the passage, Abel.'

'I'm right grateful to you, Jimpy,' Latigo said, astonished by the abilities of this man who passed himself off as a simple hostler.

'You played fair by me, Abel. I never forget a good turn, nor a bad one,' Caan replied as he mounted up and swung his horse around, as athletic and as courageous as they come.

Swinging up into the saddle, Latigo rode into the passage between the cliffs. As he went he repeatedly told himself that Anna-Maria, completely unaware of what had happened here, would be waiting patiently for him at Absaroka Peak.

★ ★ ★

Sharing a table with Barton Travers in Dinah's Diner, Casa Grande's only eatery, Marshal Steiner's meal was made tasteless by concern over what the banker had told him. If Latigo succeeded in buying the Whitsall store after taking over the Kickapoo Crogan would be enraged.

'Though I'm supporting Abel Latigo in this,' Travers continued. 'I do fear the consequences for the town. Crogan could turn our main street into a river of blood.'

'Not right now he couldn't,' Steiner advised. 'Crogan has lost too many men of late, including his best gunslingers, to do any serious damage.'

'But surely that only postpones the inevitable,' Travers remarked.

'Exactly,' Steiner said. 'Latigo has accrued much money since coming to Casa Grande, and he has shown himself to be a formidable fighter. But when it comes down to it, he is just one man, a chancer, a drifter, whose power lies only in his fists and a fast draw. Crogan has unimaginable wealth and the power to have any person of authority in the territory do his bidding.'

Travers considered this. 'So there can be only one outcome. Latigo will be the loser?'

'Yes, Barton, but the fact that he will go down fighting means big trouble.'

'Where will you stand when this confrontation happens, Brett?' Travers asked. 'You once told me that you came here to prepare for retirement.'

The marshal said with an affirmative nod, 'That was my plan.'

'A plan that can only be saved by you

taking Crogan's side,' Travers sagely observed.

'It can't survive even if I don't take sides but stick to enforcing the law, Barton.'

Seeing the logic of this, and sympathizing, Travers enquired, 'So, what will you do?'

'I just don't know,' the usually decisive marshal admitted morosely. 'Once a man like Latigo steps on to the vengeance trail, nothing will stop him.'

'You're saying he's come here purposely to get Lon Crogan?' Travers probed.

Making the lighting of a cigar into a kind of ritual, Marshal Steiner pretended not to have heard the question.

★ ★ ★

There had been no sign of Anna-Maria when Latigo had reached Absaroka Peak. He returned to town, and now followed Henry Whitsall through the store into the living quarters. Barry

Cleat had recovered sufficiently to be dressed and sitting in a chair.

Cleat covertly checked that neither Verity nor her brother was within earshot, then asked in a low tone, 'Have you been able to come up with a way to help these kids, Latigo?'

'I'm just about to make them an offer,' Latigo answered.

He was moving away when Cleat asked earnestly, 'Have you seen Anna-Maria around?'

'No.'

'I suspect that her father has ordered her to stay away from me,' Cleat said. 'Me and Anna-Maria have a kind of arrangement, you see. We've not made any actual plans yet, but it will come to that, I'm sure. But Crogan doesn't think there's any man good enough for his daughter.'

'She'll find a way to get to see you,' Latigo sympathized falsely.

'I hope that you're right.'

Latigo waited while Verity dried her hands after washing crocks in a bowl before speaking to her and her brother. 'Could the two of you spare me a few minutes in private?'

Puzzled, Verity led the way into the store. All three of them waited while Henry lit an oil lamp and replaced the globe. Then the brother and sister, their young faces showing the strain caused by their financial predicament, turned expectantly to Latigo.

'I hope that I am not interfering,' he began. 'But I know of your problem with the store.'

'Our home as well,' Verity clarified.

'I understand that, Miss Whitsall. I am also aware that despite you having paid up to date, your agreement to purchase will not be honoured by Ringstead.'

'Ben Ringstead is just a front for Crogan,' Henry corrected him.

'That's what I'm given to understand,' Latigo said. 'I have a proposition for you.'

'What is it?' Verity asked, her eagerness tempered by dread of possible disappointment.

'I would be prepared to buy the place at a fair price.'

A pleased grin spread over Henry's face. 'That would stop Crogan from getting it.'

'But it won't prevent us losing our home and everything that we've worked so hard for,' the more practical Verity, commented.

'You and Henry would remain living here and running the business,' Latigo explained.

Verity brightened up at this, before saying unhappily, 'We'd be working for you.'

'You would be working for yourselves as you are now.'

'The store isn't a gold mine, Mr Latigo,' Verity pointed out. 'Whether or not what you are proposing works depends on what share of the profits you will take.'

'Not one cent,' Latigo declared.

Awestruck, the brother and sister could only stare dumbly at him. Then Verity gathered her wits to enquire,

'Why invest your money if you want nothing in return?'

'I have my reasons. Reasons that make good sense to me.'

'Would this be a temporary arrangement?' Verity queried. 'I wouldn't want us to be spending every day wondering if you are about to change your mind and want us out.'

'There is no need ever to fear that, Verity,' Latigo replied. 'You can trust me.'

'I think that we know that,' Verity said with the trace of a smile.

'I sure do,' her brother heartily supported her.

Latigo looked from one to the other of them. 'Do we have a deal?'

'We have a deal,' Verity and Henry said in unison.

'Then tomorrow morning I'll have the papers for you to sign. You won't regret this.'

'I am sure that we won't, Mr Latigo,' Verity said, offering her small, cool hand in a businesslike handshake.

The subtle shades created by the single oil-lamp brought out a beauty in Verity that had previously escaped Latigo's notice. Their eyes met and she held his gaze for a long moment before blushing shyly and quickly looking away.

As the moment passed, Henry, unaware that it had taken place, was ready to show Latigo to the door. Out of his sister's earshot, he stammered a little as he said, 'I'm ashamed that you had to rescue me at the saloon.'

'You have no reason to be, Henry,' Latigo assured him. 'It was four against one.'

'But you beat all four,' Henry protested.

'That's not so, Henry. I'd be dead meat now but for you.'

Henry spoke modestly. 'That was just luck. I wanted to ask a favour of you. Will you teach me to handle a gun?'

Latigo looked to the back of the store where Verity was watching them, suspiciously he felt sure. He said, 'I don't think your sister would want that, Henry.'

'I'm my own man,' Henry objected. 'I want to learn how to be able to protect Verity.'

'I guess that I owe you,' Latigo said, though still having doubts. 'After the signing tomorrow morning we'll see what you can do.'

'Thank you . . . Abel,' a delighted Henry hesitated over using Latigo's first name. 'But Verity mustn't know.'

'I sort of gathered that, Henry,' Latigo said with a smile as he went out of the door.

He had only walked a few yards into the darkness of night when he saw Anna-Maria standing in the glow of a lamp outside of a cigar store. It was plain that she had seen him visit the Whitsalls, and was waiting for him.

*   *   *

Leaning with one elbow on the bar in the Lazy Horse Saloon, Jimpy Caan was surprised not to see Abel Latigo sitting at what had become his favourite poker table. Though the possibility had occurred to Jimpy that Latigo might not have returned safely from Absaroka Peak, he dismissed it as absurd. Latigo may have been pinned down that afternoon, but he was sure that he would have eventually found a way out of the situation without Jimpy's help. Latigo was a survivor.

Seeing Marshal Steiner enter the saloon with his customary caution, Jimpy turned to the barkeep and ordered a whiskey for Steiner.

'Latigo's not here,' Steiner commented, not stating the obvious but to elicit an explanation from Caan.

'No reason why he shouldn't be, Brett, s'far as I know. A couple of Crogan's men had him pinned down at the start of the passage leading to Absaroka Peak. But I helped him out.'

Steiner had no need to enquire what Caan meant by 'helped him out'. Jimpy Caan was more Cherokee than the half he claimed to be, and the two Crogan men would be dead. So he asked, 'Then Latigo came back to town with you?'

'That ain't rightly so, Brett,' Caan replied. 'The stubborn cuss was still dead set on riding on to Absaroka Peak.'

'That figures,' Steiner nodded worriedly. 'Latigo's galloping into trouble with his horse's hoofs pounding and its bridle chains rattling, Jimpy, and nothing is going to stop him.'

'Big trouble, Brett?'

'Real bad. When it happens Casa Grande will never have known anything like it.'

Fascinated, Caan asked pseudo-innocently, 'The day Latigo rode into town he wanted to know a lot about Lon Crogan.'

'Nice try, Jimpy,' Steiner said, allowing himself a tight-lipped smile. 'But you won't learn anything from me. It's best to stay out of this sort of thing.'

'Stay out of it!' Caan exclaimed in disgust. 'What in tarnation are you saying, Brett? Because of Latigo I shot two Crogan men today. How d'you say I can stay out of it?'

'By saying nothing about today. I doubt anyone knows who it was that backed Latigo out there,' Steiner advised, finishing his drink. 'I'm off on my rounds. Probably in here later, Jimpy.'

'Can't think of anywhere else I'll be,' Caan responded.

Left without company, Jimpy ordered another drink and took it with him as he wandered over to what he discovered was a tame game of cards. He was watching with casual interest, when a flustered Pastor Morrish crashed in through the doors of the saloon. Completely bewildered in an environment that was totally alien to him, the clergyman looked frantically around.

Spotting Jimpy, Morrish ran to him shouting excitedly, 'Hurry, Mr Caan, hurry. Your stables are on fire.'

★　★　★

In the dim light of the lamp Anna-Maria's eyes were a blank dark grey as she slanted a look at Latigo. 'I know you are thinking about what happened to you this afternoon.'

The cottage cloak that she wore, the hood tied under the chin of her strong-featured face, effectively added a mystique to her striking good looks. She waited, silent and unemotional, for his reaction. There was nothing for Latigo to say. If she had played no part in it, how could she know that something had happened to him?

He said as neutrally as the situation would allow, 'The way it seems to me, Anna-Maria, is that I told no one other than Brett Steiner that I was going to meet you, but two men with rifles were waiting for me.'

'It wasn't Marshal Steiner.'

'I know that.'

'I don't think that you'll believe me if I tell you what happened,' she said, her voice barely rising above a whisper.

'Does it matter to you whether I

believe you or not?' Latigo asked.

'It matters very much.'

Latigo had a problem with her answer. There was no way he could accept that the self-sufficient Anna-Maria cared about anyone's opinion of her. Neither could he envisage how any person other than Anna-Maria could be responsible for the situation he had ridden into that afternoon. Yet there was some magic about being in her presence that prevented him from walking away.

'I'm listening, if you want to tell me,' he said.

Hesitating, she began. 'It's difficult. You see I — '

Anna-Maria broke off in mid-sentence as the darkness that had closed around them was suddenly brightened by a bright-orange light. Smelling smoke at same time, Latigo stepped out into the street and looked to his right where long tongues of flame were licking at the night sky.

Getting his mental map of the town right, Latigo identified the source of the flames. 'That's Jimpy Caan's place ablaze.'

'I stabled Caesar there when I came into town,' Anna-Maria cried, distress boosting the volume of her voice.

Latigo started off at a sprint and then slowed to allow her to keep pace. When they were still some distance away the seriousness of the fire was evident. A human chain along which buckets of water were being passed was already working as Latigo and Anna-Maria ran up.

'Has anyone fetched the horses out?' she shouted at a man running by them, but he was in too much of a panic to hear her question, let alone reply to it.

They saw Caan then. The sleeve of his jacket burning, he was leading a terrified horse out of the blazing building.

'That's not Caesar.'

Latigo heard Anna-Maria's cry of despair as he ran from her towards Caan. He shouted, 'Are there any more in there, Jimpy?'

'Just two, Abel,' Jimpy called back. He added. 'It's not safe to go back in now.'

Ignoring the warning, Latigo dashed into the building. He paused inside to peer through dense smoke. Then he moved further in to find the smoke replaced by flames that enabled him to see. Ahead were two horses kicking and screaming in terror. One of them had to be Caesar, and Latigo was hurrying towards them when he sensed someone behind him. It was Caan.

'What are you doing in here, Jimpy?'

'Taking care of you,' Caan replied coolly as he and Latigo tried to calm and release the horses. 'Maybe the time will come when I want to stake you in another game of poker.'

Laughing at the hostler's courageous sense of humour as they got the pair of horses something like under control, Latigo seized what he recognized as Caesar, and Caan grabbed the other horse. They were within a few yards of the door when a burning beam crashed down from roof. It hit the rear of the horse Caan was leading. The animal reared up, knocking Caan backwards. His head cracked against a post, and Latigo saw him collapse unconscious on to the hot ashes that carpeted the ground.

Having to fight both horses, Latigo somehow managed to get them to the door and out of the blazing building. A man grabbed the second horse, while Anna-Maria, crying in relief, clasped Caesar round the neck with both arms. Latigo heard her cry out, pleading with him not to go back into what was now an inferno. But he carried on, coughing and choking on thicker smoke as he ran blindly to where he had seen Caan fall.

Though having partially regained consciousness, Caan hadn't come round sufficiently to be able to move. Bending, Latigo used both arms to lift the stunned man up over his shoulder and began a run for the door. Before he had staggered a few feet under Caan's weight, a section of the roof of the building crashed down in front of him, creating a wall of fire. There was no way out.

Still with the unconscious Caan on his shoulder, Latigo heard Brett Steiner shout above the roar of blazing wood, 'Can you hear me, Latigo?'

'I can hear you, Marshal,' Latigo, now finding it difficult to breathe, called back.

'We've an iron hook wedged in the front of the building with a cable attached to two horses,' Steiner shouted. 'We are ready to pull the wall away, but need your say-so, because we could bring the whole building down on top of you.'

'Go ahead, Steiner. I've nothing to lose.'

His clothing scorching and his lungs feeling about to burst, Latigo waited. He could hear shouting outside, but couldn't tell what was being said. Then the burning timber facing him shuddered a little and he heard what was left of the roof creaking above him. The wall of flaming wood started to move gradually away from him, as the groaning of the roof became louder.

Men were shouting and women were screaming outside as the blazing wall was hauled away from the building. Burning timbers broke away, twisting dangerously through the air before crashing to the ground to send sparks flying high. Getting a glimpse of the night sky, Latigo shifted Caan's body to a more comfortable position on his shoulder as he prepared to run.

A mighty roar from above drowned the shouts of encouragement from outside. Looking up, Latigo saw that the roof was now well alight and close to collapsing. He ran through the dying flames of the falling timber, leaping over obstacles as the cracking and breaking away of the roof grew into a crescendo. With Latigo having just a short distance to go to be safely outside, the roof imploded with a deafening sound. With rafters falling behind him, Latigo threw himself and Caan out into the night.

As he hit the ground there was pandemonium among the spectators as the stables completely disintegrated behind him. Bruised by his fall, Latigo came up on to his knees, coughing and wheezing. He laid Caan on his back and checked him over. Doc Hendly dropped to one knee beside him to take over the task.

Getting shakily to his feet, Latigo was aware of Verity Whitsall, concern for him on her face and with her lame leg dragging, coming towards him. He was mystified when she suddenly stopped. He knew why then as Anna-Maria came up beside him to clasp his arm with both hands. Before the little female drama between the two had been fully played out, Jimpy Caan surprised everyone by opening his eyes and speaking loudly to Latigo.

'Are you all right, Abel?'

'Mighty fine,' Latigo assured him. 'Worry about yourself, *amigo*. Let the doc fix you up.'

Ignoring this advice, Caan painfully

propped himself up on one elbow to view his ruined stables. He said, 'You know who did this, and why, Abel. He knows that I was with you out Absaroka Peak way today, and wanted to get even. That lowdown stinking scalawag Lonroy Crogan, that's who.'

A shocked murmur ran through the crowd. Regretting that Anna-Maria had heard Caan's public condemnation of her father, Latigo realized that she no longer held his arm. Turning his head, he found that she had disappeared into the night. Imagining the profound shame Anna-Maria had to be feeling, Latigo felt an immense sympathy for her. Verity stood a short distance away, undecided. Marshal Steiner was striding towards him.

Steiner congratulated him. 'This would have been a whole heap worse tonight without you, Abel.'

'Without me it wouldn't have happened,' Latigo commented morbidly.

9

Early in the morning following the fire, Latigo made his way on foot to the premises of Doc Hendly. A liking for Jimpy Caan, together with the knowledge that he was, albeit unwittingly, responsible for what was obviously an arson attack on Caan's stables, had him worried about the hostler. Slightly disorientated from being awoken from a deep sleep, the doctor looked twice his considerable age as he stood in his doorway peering at Latigo. Though assuring Latigo that Caan was suffering from nothing more than minor bruising and singed eyebrows, there was an uncharacteristic shiftiness to Doc Hendly that made Latigo suspicious.

'Was he here at your place overnight, Doc?' he enquired. When Hendly gave an affirmative nod, Latigo glanced to the east where dawn was streaking the sky with first red and then gold, and asked, 'So, he's still here now.'

'Yes. Well, not really. No,' Hendly stammered, confused by his own evasiveness.

'Then where is he, Doc?'

Taking a long time to reply, the doctor eventually did speak, but reluctantly. 'Jimpy's mad enough about being burnt out to swallow a horned-toad backwards. He rode out before sun-up. Heading for the LC Ranch, I guess.'

Alarmed at hearing this, Latigo hurried to where he had the previous evening left his horse in the small yard at the side of the Whitsall store. Saddling up first, he hammered hard on the store's door while it was still barely daylight. After he had banged on the door with his fist a second time, a sleepy Henry opened the door.

Blinking in an effort to clear the sleep from his eyes, Henry took a few seconds to recognize Latigo. 'What's happened?'

'Nothing to concern you, Henry,' Latigo replied hurriedly. 'I have to go out of town right now. When the bank's open, you and Verity get yourselves down there and tell Barton Travers that you want to sign the papers he's prepared for me. I'll do my signing when I get back.'

'Where are you going?' Henry called.

Latigo, going to his horse, didn't answer.

A heavy early-morning mist shrouded the terrain as he took the trail along which he had followed Anna-Maria Crogan at night. The only sound was the faint rippling of a nearby stream. His main worry was how long a head start Caan had on him. Though Jimpy had proved himself to be more than capable with a rifle, no man could ride into Crogan's fortress of a ranch alone and survive.

Having lost his livelihood last night, Jimpy Caan was about to lose his life in an anger-fuelled, ill-considered crusade for revenge.

Reaching the spur of volcanic rock where he had come upon Anna-Maria, Latigo heard Anna-Maria's voice from that night when she had told him, 'We have less than two miles to go.' Latigo judged that Caan was so far ahead that he would reach the LC Ranch before he could catch up with him. That presented him with a big problem. Rescuing Caan could well prove impossible once he had passed through the ranch gates. Yet Latigo refused to give up, just as he knew that Jimpy wouldn't desert him had their situations been reversed. Lightly spurring his horse, he moved on.

A few minutes later he reined up as in the distance he saw a rider descending a long hill, the horse moving at a leisurely pace. Like Latigo, the rider was heading for the LC Ranch, but from a different angle. Being lower and shielded from sight by the terrain, Latigo was also closer to the ranch. Aware of the possibility that, depending on who the rider was, he might use him to his own advantage, Latigo rode to a cluster of tall rocks. Dismounting and concealing his horse, he climbed a rock and sat on his heels, waiting.

Watching the rider join the trail that would have him pass the rocks, every muscle in Latigo's body tensed, every nerve he possessed tingled as he recognized the approaching horseman from the way he sat in the saddle. There could be no mistake. It was Major Lonroy Crogan.

★   ★   ★

Psychologically refreshed by his daily visit to the hill, Crogan was planning the day ahead as he returned home. Losing out on the Kickapoo Saloon had initially been painful for him, but now he had relegated it to the category of a minor setback. Ringstead, who'd had his instructions to ensure that nothing similar should ever again happen, would be coming to the ranch to report later in the day. Whoever this sidewinder Latigo was, he had had his moment of glory. He was about to discover that no one takes liberties with Lonroy Crogan.

He was passing through Thunder Rocks, close enough to home to feel perfectly secure, when the blood seemed to freeze painfully in his veins as a terse command came from behind him.

'Rein up, and stay looking straight ahead.'

In no doubt that there was a gun aimed at him, Crogan obeyed. He felt fear and fury alternating in him rapidly as his reins were taken from his hand. From the corner of his eye he could see them being slashed by a knife.

'Keep looking ahead and get down from your horse and put your hands behind your back.'

Insult was added to ignominy for Crogan as he felt his wrists being tied agonizingly tightly with his own reins. Then two hands came from behind to place what he assumed was a necker-chief across his eyes. As the world went black for him, a knot was tied tightly at the back of his head.

With a hand on one of his arms, his captor moved him closer to his horse, saying, 'You'll find this a mite difficult, but once you get one foot in a stirrup you can swing yourself up into the saddle.'

Humiliated by several failed attempts to mount up, falling this way and that, Crogan no longer felt even a slight trace of fear. Now he was in the grip of a rage such as he had never before known. Suspecting that it was Latigo who had jumped him, he made himself a fervent promise that the man would die. But doubt was creeping in about it being Latigo. The fact that he had been blind-folded must mean that he knew his captor. Yet he couldn't recognize the voice. What made it all worse was that he could detect that the other man, whoever he was, had difficulty in stifling his amusement at his clumsy attempts to get up into the saddle.

'Try again,' his tormentor ordered.

'Make it this time, or I'll shoot you in both knees and drape you over the saddle.'

Accepting this as no idle threat, Crogan sweated profusely as his foot found a stirrup. Unable to reach up to grip the saddle, pain and discomfort came close to disabling him as with a superhuman effort he got himself up on his horse. He came close to immediately toppling off, but by some miracle stayed put.

'Right. I'll be right behind you with a Colt pointing at your back. Move your horse off at a walk when I tell you, and guide it with your knees.'

Almost unseated by the jolt of his mount's first movement, Crogan felt fear again as he rode blindly into the unknown.

★ ★ ★

A six-gun held in his right hand, Latigo enjoyed the power he held at that moment over the man he had hated for so long. They rounded the low hill he remembered and entered the miniature valley. Up ahead were the ranch gates, outside of which stood two men. Both of them brought up their rifles as Latigo and his captive approached.

Making a menacing gesture towards Crogan with his Colt, Latigo told the two men, 'Drop your rifles.'

When the pair had obeyed the order, he said, 'Now unbuckle your gunbelts with your left hands and let them fall to the ground.'

The two men slowly and carefully did as they were told. Then they looked up at Latigo in fear of what might happen next.

'Is Jimpy Caan here at the ranch?' Latigo enquired.

Not replying the two men first looked at each other, then turned plaintively to Crogan, as if the blindfolded man could see their predicament and help them. Moving his horse two paces closer to Crogan, Latigo aimed his gun at the back of his captive's head. The move was a deciding factor for one of the hired hands, a short, fat man with bowed legs.

'Yes. He rode in all riled up like, and Billy Kline, our foreman, has tied him tight to the corral till he cools down.'

Lowering his gun and jabbing it into the middle of Crogan's back, Latigo gave the bow-legged cowboy instructions. 'You mount up and ride to the ranch. Free Caan and put him on his horse and ride back here with him. Bring anyone else with you and I'll blow a hole right through the middle of your boss. You got that?'

With a curt nod to signal that he understood, the Crogan man walked to his horse, mounted up and rode off. The remaining cowboy, a surly, gangling fellow, frowned as he studied Latigo wonderingly, then reached a decision and said, 'You're this Latigo, ain't you?'

Aware of Crogan giving a little jolt of surprise on hearing this, Latigo didn't give the cowboy an answer. All of them remained silent from then on. A silence that was broken a short while later by the pounding of horses' hoofs. An alert Latigo listened carefully until he was certain that there were only two riders. Then the cowboy rode up with Jimpy Caan riding beside him.

'I kinda thought you'd turn up,' Caan grinned at Latigo. 'I guess I made a danged fool of myself trying to take on the whole LC Ranch.'

'Get moving, Jimpy,' Latigo said. He indicated the two cowboys with his free hand. 'Get rid of their weapons and their horses.'

'Sure thing,' Caan chuckled, dismounting and picking up a rifle. Aiming it at the cowboy who had remained on his horse, he ordered 'Get down, pronto.'

The rider hurriedly dismounted. Throwing the horse's reins over its head, Caan slapped it hard on the rump. It galloped away as he walked to the other horse and repeated the process. Then he picked up the two discarded gunbelts and draped them over the horn of his saddle. Catching hold of the barrel of the rifle that he had picked up, he swung the weapon and smashed the stock against a rock. Doing the same to the second rifle, he swung up lithely into the saddle.

'We're ready to hit the trail,' he reported to Latigo.

They moved off in the direction of Casa Grande, with Caan in the lead and Latigo riding behind the still bound and blindfolded Crogan. When they reached the spur of volcanic rock where Anna-Maria's horse had gone lame, Latigo called to Caan:

'This will do, Jimpy. We'll leave him here.'

With a dubious expression on his face, Caan asked, 'You gonna free his wrists? I ain't got no good reason to like this critter, but it don't seem somehow right to leave any man tied and blindfolded out here.'

'He'll soon be found, Jimpy,' Latigo reassured his friend. 'His men will be hot on our trail right now. Just hitch his horse to that needle of rock there.'

'I guess you're right,' Caan agreed as he tethered Crogan's horse.

Crogan uttered not one word when they left him. On the way back to Casa Grande they spotted a rider heading towards them. Leaving the trail to conceal themselves and their horses in a group of trees, they waited for the horseman to pass. It was Ben Ringstead heading for the LC Ranch.

'He's about to meet Lon Crogan earlier than expected,' Caan chuckled.

* * *

'I know it's a poor second to owning the place,' Barry Cleat sympathized with Verity, 'but you and Henry are still here running the store.'

'That's what Mr Travers said,' Verity nodded.

Though initially mollified by Latigo's offer, the act of adding her and her brother's names to the deed had a tremendous significance. It seemed to Verity that in penning their signatures they had signed their lives away. The endless number of days, the long hours spent toiling in the store, now amounted to nothing. The comfortable, meaningful future that they had worked so hard for had vanished.

Having recovered sufficiently to be able to move around, albeit carefully, Cleat placed a comforting hand on the girl's thin shoulder. 'I pride myself on being a pretty good judge of character, Verity, and I'd say that Abel Latigo is as straight as they come. There may well come a time when you will be able to buy the store back from him. I'm sure that he'll be happy to assist you when that opportunity comes.'

'If ever,' Verity said despondently. 'But, yes, I know that he is acting in our interest. I was wrong about him when he came here first. It's just that everything that was so positive and reliable seems so uncertain now.' She paused abruptly and apologized. 'I am so sorry, Barry. I'm complaining to you about my problems when I know that you are awfully worried about Anna-Maria.'

'I want to help you and Henry as much as I can.' Cleat smiled at her. 'Her father has to be the reason for Anna-Maria not coming here. But she'll find a way soon, I am confident of that.'

'You two are very close,' Verity remarked shyly.

'I'll let you into a little secret, Verity. Ken Wharton, my foreman, is doing an excellent job now. He's probably running things better than I would be managing if the shooting hadn't happened. But being here has given me the chance to reflect, to see what I was doing wrong. I was too intense, Verity, too closely involved with the business. Things will be different from now on. When I can get back to my business and secure its future, I am going to ask Anna-Maria to be my wife.'

He looked so happy as he contemplated his proposal that Verity discovered she was involuntarily offering up a silent prayer for him and Anna-Maria. Then she realized that in automatically responding with prayer she had confirmed how desperate was the present situation in Casa Grande.

* * *

Taking a bottle from a ponderous early-Victorian black walnut cabinet, Lonroy Crogan poured three drinks. Passing one to Ben Ringstead, and another to Billy Kline, he raised his own glass high as if about to propose a toast. But he changed his mind and put the glass to his lips. Not saying a word, he drank long and deep.

Crogan had been unusually taciturn since being rescued by Ringstead and meeting a search party led by Kline on the way back to the ranch. Now Kline, displaying his habitual deference while in the presence of Crogan, sipped his drink and kept his eyes downcast. Ringstead, being of superior intellect to the ranch foreman, covertly studied Crogan so as to predict what to expect and plan how to deal with it when it occurred. Crogan's normally tanned face was white from suppressed rage. Releasing the index finger of the hand holding his glass, he pointed at Ringstead.

'It is definite that the Whitsalls have sold out to Latigo?'

'The deal is done, Lonroy. It happened before I knew anything about it.'

Emptying his glass, Crogan turned his back on the other two men as he poured himself another drink, then spun round purposely to face them. He addressed Kline. 'Who is your finest horseman, Billy?'

'Pedro Sanchez. There's no doubt about that, Mr Crogan.'

'Then he has a long ride, a fast ride. Go tell him to prepare to leave for Wichita within the hour.'

When his foreman had hurried out of the house, Crogan refilled Ringstead's glass before saying in a deceptively mild tone, 'I'm through playing games with Latigo. It's time for action, Ben. I'm sending Sanchez to Wichita to hire the Harlan brothers.'

'What about Marshal Steiner, Lonroy?' Ringstead enquired.

'What about Steiner?'

'He's not likely to take kindly to the three most notorious hired guns in the territory riding into his town,' Ringstead reasoned.

'My town,' Crogan corrected him bitingly. 'It will be time for Brett Steiner to make up his mind when the Harlans ride in.'

'Steiner is a proud man, Lonroy.'

'Steiner is over the hill, and can no longer afford pride,' Crogan said confidently as he walked over to sit in and be engulfed by his Sleepy Hollow armchair.

Knowing Crogan's daily routine as well as he did his own, Ringstead accepted that his visit was over. Crogan's eyelids were slowly dropping, announcing that his afternoon nap had begun. Ringstead made his way quietly to the door.

★   ★   ★

Having stood in the doorway of her room listening to the conversation, Anna-Maria stepped back but kept the door ajar. A virtual prisoner in the house, she was made distraught by the conviction that Latigo regarded her as a conspirator in a plot to have him shot. That was far from the truth. Worried by the tense situation that was building up in the area, she had genuinely wanted to meet Latigo in the hope of learning what was happening. Seeing her leave the ranch the previous afternoon, her father, believing that she was heading for town to see Barry Cleat, had Kline follow her.

On discovering that she was on the trail to Absaroka Peak, the sycophantic Kline had caught up with her and taken her back to the ranch. Her father's obsessional suspicion of Latigo had him send out two men with rifles in the belief, which happened to be correct, that it would be Latigo coming through the pass.

Since going into town on the night Caan's stables burned down to explain to Latigo about not meeting him, she had not left the LC Ranch. Latigo had exacerbated her father's habitual, underlying mistrust of people to the extent that he had come to mistrust her. Now, through the crack of the almost closed door of her room, she saw Ben Ringstead come out into the hall. The fact that he looked perplexed made it easier for her to broach the subject. Though they never showed disloyalty, her father's associates were often profoundly disturbed by his actions.

Stepping out into the hall, she said, 'I overheard some of your discussion with my father, and what he intends to do worries me greatly.'

'It worries me too, Miss Anna-Maria,' Ringstead confessed. 'But there would seem nothing that we can do. For some reason that I suspect even he doesn't understand, your father is reacting strangely to this Latigo fellow.'

'Are these men he is hiring as dangerous as I imagine them to be?'

Though it was her father's doing, Anna-Maria couldn't stand the thought of an unsuspecting man being attacked by three killers. She was surprised to find it was even more difficult to contemplate when the man in question was Abel Latigo.

'Worse than anything you can imagine, Miss Anna-Maria,' Ringstead replied. 'To bring the three Harlan brothers to Casa Grande is to endanger the lives of every man, woman, and child in the town.'

'Then we must do something to prevent that happening,' a horrified Anna-Maria insisted.

'There is nothing we can do.'

'I am sure that Latigo would leave town if he knew. That would mean everything would go back to normal.

Could you tell him what my father plans, Mr Ringstead?'

With a negative shake of his head, Ringstead said, 'I can't do that for two reasons. First is because of my business relationship with your father. Second is that I have met Latigo only as a card player. Otherwise I know nothing of the man.'

'I have met him,' Anna-Maria said. 'He is not an unreasonable man. I feel sure that if you explained the situation he would be willing to help.'

'With respect, you are simplifying the matter,' Ringstead advised. 'Your father has concluded that Latigo is deliberately conducting some sort of campaign against him. I must say that there is evidence more than to suggest that this is the case. That being so, any appeal we may attempt to Latigo would prove ineffective.'

'Is there anything that you can suggest?'

'As I share your concern at the way things are shaping up, I am prepared to have a word with Brett Steiner.'

'I am not sure that will help, but thank you,' Anna-Maria said.

Opening the door to leave, Ringstead paused to issue a warning. 'As far as your father is concerned, this conversation between you and me did not take place.'

Confident that she would agree, Ringstead went out without waiting for her answer.

★ ★ ★

Shocked by what she had seen, Verity turned quickly away from the store's side window. Out in the yard her brother was wearing a gunbelt and Abel Latigo was instructing him on the fast-draw. Gripping the counter, she felt physically sick. On the frontier it had been necessary to adapt to violence, but Verity never could, nor ever would, accept it. Her ever-present dread was that Henry's tendency for hero worship would lead to him taking up the gun.

That day had come, and she was determined to put a stop to it.

When Henry, no longer wearing a gunbelt, came in through the side door with Latigo, she called to him. 'Henry, we are out of molasses, please fetch some from out back.'

'Mr Latigo,' she began when her brother had left, choosing her words carefully. 'We are most grateful to you for your help with the store, and I don't wish to cause offence. Henry is an excellent storekeeper, but he is not cut out to be a gunfighter. I don't know how to say this, but I'd prefer you not to encourage him in the way I saw you doing just a short while ago.'

'That's put me in a real difficult position, Verity,' Latigo said ruefully. 'I like Henry, and couldn't refuse when he asked me to show him how to handle a gun. He is a quick learner. I am sure this is just the high spirits of a young man, and your brother has no interest whatsoever in becoming a gunslinger.'

'Nevertheless, it is a step in a

direction that I don't want Henry to take.'

'It is a step that I often regret having taken myself,' Latigo admitted solemnly. 'Yet Henry is so keen to learn that I'd hate to disappoint him. He is a level-headed boy, Verity, and he wants to learn gunplay so as to be able to protect you should it be necessary. You have my word that I'll discourage him should he think about putting his new skill to a wrong use.'

★   ★   ★

Longing for a return of the peaceful and less problematic pre-Latigo evenings, Marshal Steiner wearily and worriedly began his round in the Lazy Horse. It was still early and no games of chance had commenced. Seeing Latigo at the bar, Steiner walked over to him.

'Relax, Marshal,' Latigo spread his arms wide in a gesture of innocence. 'I haven't started any trouble, neither do I intend to.'

'You don't have to start it. Trouble follows you as close as a shadow,' Steiner complained.

Buying the marshal a drink, Latigo pushed the glass towards him, asking jocularly, 'What haven't I done now?'

'Seems like Crogan is planning a showdown with you.'

'Then he'll have to show a whole lot more courage than he did at Shiloh and Chicamauga,' Latigo commented wryly.

'Crogan relies on money, not courage. He's hiring the Harlan brothers to deal with you.'

As he said this, Steiner studied Latigo closely for a reaction, but Latigo's facial expression and eyes registered no change. That confirmed for the marshal what he had dreaded. Unafraid, Latigo would face the Harlans. That was bad news for Casa Grande and for its town marshal.

'This is my play, Steiner, so there is no reason for you to get involved,' Latigo said.

'My job means that I am involved.'

'You could make sure that you're out of town when the Harlans get here.'

Steiner put his glass on the bar. He spoke as he was moving away. 'I'll be here if it happens, Latigo. I was hoping that you would have the good sense not to be.'

Looking down at the glass, Latigo was puzzled to see that Steiner had left most of the whiskey, in it untouched. Then he remembered the marshal once telling him that he wouldn't drink with a man it was likely he would have to kill.